THE BURGH AND THE BEES

PLANTED AND PLOWED
BOOK 2

LAINEY DAVIS

ABOUT THIS BOOK

I'm living proof you can't fix a broken heart with a hammer.

After losing my dad, I inherited his construction business alongside a heap of trouble. Enter Eden Storm: a bee-charming beauty who's got me questioning my mistakes and pleading for a second chance.

I met her at rock bottom and I really can't afford to get stung with my business teetering on the edge right now. Eden's life is no garden, either, with a swarm of sisters and her own business on the rocks. She doesn't need to renovate me, too. Can I construct a happy ending for us, or will my past mistakes come back to sting us both?

The Burgh and the Bees is book two of the Planted and Plowed series of romantic comedies starring the Storm sisters. Love blooms reluctantly and stems get spliced in these steamy books full of small-town swoon in a big-city setting

1

EDEN

I NEED to ignore the screaming. I have to find my zen, or these bees are going to *really* start stinging, and the last thing I want is more bees getting hurt.

I pull my veil from my bag and slide it over my head. There goes the easy breathing, but hey, that's the price I pay for what I do. The bride isn't the only one wearing a veil at this wedding. A smile touches the corners of my mouth as I march toward the swarm in the church garden.

I SET down the modified cardboard box I brought with me, hoping it's large enough to transport the little critters out of this inhospitable environment.

A child runs past me, swatting and screaming, and I want to glare at their mother, but it's more important I find the queen and get this colony to safety.

I pat my pocket to make sure I have my queen clip. I stoop to gather my box, and I make my way toward the picnic table where the shrieking pastor told me a colony of bees have taken up temporary residence. When it's time to make babies, some bees leave their hives, and well, sometimes they get a little lost. I can relate.

"Hey, friends," I whisper, crouching beside the table to study the situation. I want to get a sense of how long the bees have been here, if the queen started laying eggs or building honeycomb yet.

People have mostly stopped screaming, but the garden vibrates with nervous energy. A man's voice drifts through my bubble of concentration. "Shouldn't you be blowing smoke at them? Shouldn't she have smoke?"

I close my eyes and take a deep breath, turning my head toward the voice. "Please stay back while I'm working with the bees. I need to find the queen so I can get you all to your party."

The murmurs of human voices blend with the buzz of the bees' wings, and I get myself in the zone. "Let's try that again, gals. I'm Eden Storm. I'm going to take care of you, okay?" I tilt my head, searching. The bees have not yet formed any significant comb in the wooden table. They've only been here a few hours. I reach toward a busy cluster of bees, guessing the queen is in here, surrounded by her hardworking attendants. What a life.

"Eh, not really," I say out loud. The queen would have had to destroy her sisters to take the throne, and since my sisters are my whole world... I can't even think about it.

"There you are!" I whisper-shout to the group of bees, reaching into my pocket for the clip. If I can get the queen into my temporary hive, the rest of the bees will follow.

Except maybe the drones. They're busy finding other queens to boink and keep the species going.

"I'm not going to hurt you," I whisper as a teenage girl wails about spraying and getting rid of them with poison. The queen nestles into the clip and pride swells in my chest. "There you go, girl," I say, placing the clip on a mended wooden frame, securing it with a rubber band. Not a minute later, the colony jets to their new home. A few stragglers buzz around completely lost, so I give them a little help, scooping them up and directing them to their leader. "I got you," I tell a particularly stubborn group, catching the last bit and settling them inside the box. I make sure they're all at ease, wiggling in content, before placing the lid over the frames. My knees creak as I rise from my crouch, and my gaze darks around to make sure I didn't miss any of the cute little workers. When the only buzz left in the air is from the box, I remove my veil and take a much-needed breath of warm summer air.

I turn to the new sound of all the wedding guests applauding, pumping their fists. A few partygoers hold bags of ice to sting wounds. I refrain from telling them a bit of baking soda is most likely all they need. They seem happy now that the bees are contained, and I always like it when people are happy.

I turn to the pastor. "I'll send you an invoice Monday morning. I'll give these gals a few minutes to load the whole colony into the box, and then I'll be out of your hair."

Blinking, mouth moving open and shut, the pastor eventually finds his voice. "That was amazing, young lady."

"Oh, I'm not that young," I blurt. I'm not terribly *old* at twenty-five, but my sisters and I basically raised ourselves, and I've had adult responsibilities for a long, long time.

Plus, it wasn't *that* amazing. I do this every day.

The bride rushes forward and throws her arms around me. "Thank you, thank you, thank you," she says, punctuating each phrase with a pumping squeeze. She is not a bride who worries about her gown getting dirty. I'm sort of glad I didn't put on my white beekeeping suit today. I would never want to upstage a bride at her own wedding. The veil was enough.

I wiggle from her hold with as much grace as I can. "It was my pleasure." This is true. I find so much joy and peace working with bees. Everything about them fascinates me, and I know it's a rare thing that they don't sting or seem to get angry with me the way they do other beekeepers. If I had a mom offering platitudes, she might say I was born to do this.

Instead, I've got sisters, and they joke that I'm a witch, but I know they admire my work.

I turn to the cardboard bee box. Almost all the bees have moved inside. "Well," I say to the crowd at large, "I better kick these guys out of your party." I often feel like I'm on the cusp of leaving a party. This swell of pride from rescuing the wedding reception? It won't last. When I get home, my sister Eila will still move out, like this colony of bees. And I'll be left behind.

Someone outside the group of wedding guests catches my attention. A man from the house next door frowns at the scene, muscular arms crossed over his chest, blond hair blowing a bit in the gentle breeze that has thankfully relieved some of the heat. No wonder these bees left their cozy hive to make babies. It's got to be ninety-five degrees out here.

But the man...

I know that man. He looks a lot better now than he did the last time I saw him, which is saying something, because he was really freaking fine that night. He squints his blue eyes, like he's trying to remember who I am. My lips pull downward. I don't want anything to do with him, thank you very much. I stash my box in the back of my van, opening all the windows in case any of the hive wants to leave.

"I'm going to turn on the AC for you," I tell the bees, turning on the engine and pulling onto Chislett Street. I see my one-night-stand-turned-disaster walk back into the house, like he doesn't know who I am. Whatever.

My eyes flick to the near-empty gas tank. Thank heavens I got this call today. It's been slow going---making a name for myself here in Pittsburgh. Don't know how I'm going to make rent now that Eila is moving in with her boyfriend. I park the van and set the new colony as far as I can from my regular hives. They need to hang out for a bit so I can make sure nobody has mites.

A moment after I stash my gear in the mudroom, my sister thunders down the stairs, holding a lamp and a giant ficus plant. "Hey, you're back. Did you get cake?"

I shake my head. "I didn't ask."

Eila huffs. "They should have offered. It's like the least they could do when you're saving their wedding from a swarm of bees."

"I would have had to stick around until they cut the cake, silly." I open the fridge and hold myself back from pouring the cold water directly from the pitcher into my mouth. I manage to get it into a glass first and guzzle it down while Eila makes another trip upstairs.

"Hey," she says, coming down with another plant under one arm and a dozen pairs of overalls over her other. "Can I borrow the van? Are you done for the day?"

"Yeah," I say, "but it needs gas." Her question takes me back to the end of my gig at the wedding reception, where I caught sight of Nate Donovan. The last time I saw him, he asked a similar question. "*Are we done here?*"

I swallow the ice water and study my sister, who's been my roommate for the past seven years. I am happy she found love, and I know she'll be back, because her beloved hops crop is growing on the lot next door. I toss her the keys from my pocket, not sure why all this is so hard. It's not like my sister is moving to another time zone. I need to figure out how to shake this off and get into my groove.

2

NATE

PEOPLE ARE SCREAMING OUTSIDE. I set down the plans I was studying and peek outside to see what the commotion is.

My guys trickle out of the house, pulling off safety gear to get a better peek at the situation in the church garden. Sparky, my welder, claps a ham-sized hand on my shoulder and squints through the chaos. "Donny, what the hell is that racket?" A sharp pang knocks the breath out of me. He called me my father's nickname. I rarely shorten my last name, Donovan, the way Dad always did. But then, his first name was Albert.

Sparky doesn't notice me having a moment. He frowns at the church. "You think they got bees over there?"

At the word bees, my crew bolts inside, slamming the door. I could tell them there's not much point, since half the windows are busted in this dump of a house. But I'm intrigued.

I once knew a beekeeper, but I stung her with bad decisions and messed everything up.

I lean against the rotting porch and try to see if this bee charmer is *my* bee charmer. A wave of shame rushes through me, hotter than the summer air, at the memory of the angry voicemail I got a year ago. A woman named Eden Storm called me every name in the book and told me I gave her the clap.

The bee whisperer next door takes off her veil, and I know it's her. She has a full head of dark hair. It's in a ponytail today, but the night I met her, she had it down in gorgeous waves. I remember meeting her; I remember her telling me she's a beekeeper. Everything after that is just fog. I got so damn drunk I don't even remember taking that gorgeous woman to bed.

God, she's stunning—petite and toned, tanned skin dark eyes. What kind of lowlife could forget anything about *her*?

"Hey, Donny, ask you something?" My foreman, Chris, pokes his head out of one of the empty window frames.

I don't turn to face him, staring intently at the bee situation and the woman wrangling all the chaos. "What's up, Chris?"

"You really want to say yes to this mess? They'd be better knocking it down and starting fresh. That's my professional opinion. Total gut job..." Chris has a heavy Pittsburgh accent. It reminds me of my dad.

I lace my fingers together behind my head, the porch sagging a bit as I give it my weight. This "gut jawb," as Chris pronounces it, will indeed be a lot of work. But it will also cover the finances of Dad's construction business—*my* construction business—for six months if it goes well. The whole thing makes me uneasy, but I figure that's either because the house is next to the church where I started going to grief support meetings, or because it's the first real project I'm starting since Dad died last spring.

All the other stuff was already in the books. This property would be new. The house is one of the three-story beauties in the Morningside neighborhood, with huge windows from the 1920s, brick exterior, and a chimney that's about to fall over. The owner is one of those out-of-town assholes who read that Pittsburgh real estate is hot right now. He wants it flipped as fast and cheap as possible. I don't need Chris to tell me that's not how Dad did business. It's not how I want to build a name for myself, either.

But I burned a lot of bridges last year in the name of grief. I drank too much. I slept around. I let a lot of people down. The fact is, I'm lucky to have been offered this job, but I can't tell that to Chris or Sparky or any of the other guys who depend on me to keep their kids fed.

Next door, a bride hugs Eden, both of them with veils tucked under their arms, and people seem to be singing Eden praises. She deserves it. She just bare-handed a chunk of bees the way I sometimes reach into a bag of pea gravel. I watch as she picks up her box full of bees like it's not a bomb. Like it's a regular box of tools or something normal. She catches me staring, and I don't avert my gaze in time to avoid her expression turning angry.

No... not angry.

Eden is *disgusted*. She storms to a van, sets the bees inside, and drives off.

I shake my head, turning my attention from where Eden burned rubber out of here. The scent of tobacco reaches my nose, and I follow it to Chris, leaning out the window, blowing a plume of smoke into the air. His face is trained on the exact spot Eden turned the corner.

I rap my knuckles on the gut jawb porch. "Yeah, Chris. We're taking the job." My tone doesn't leave room for discussion, although I wish he'd talk me out of it. "It's got good insides. It just needs a little love on the exterior, is all."

Chris snorts and stubs out his cigarette on the brick around the window. "Sure, the exterior. And the plaster. And the plumbing."

"You got somewhere better to work?"

He waves a hand at me and ducks inside. I run a palm along one of the columns on the porch. A little mortar will stabilize these bricks, and we aren't afraid of pulling out plaster to put up drywall. I think we can save this house. I can't change what I did last year when everything was raw, but maybe I can take this old beauty of a house and make it shine again.

3

EDEN

My sisters are incredible.

I'm not saying that because I'm biased. We're visiting the Homewood Cemetery today for Eila's big event, celebrating her work as the staff horticulturist. Who even knew there were horticulturists at cemeteries?

Eila knew. And she got our baby sister Eva in on the action with social media marketing. My oldest sister, Esther, mixed some fancy cocktails for the event, and Eliza has her goats there munching invasive weeds on the hillside, so they don't strangle the old headstones and damage them. Or something.

Eila has everyone from the Storm family helping to make this event shine. Well, not quite all of us, but it's still a spectacular day. Everyone is happy. *More* than happy. This is a day of celebration.

My sisters seem to have moved past our upbringing and processed the neglect. Eila even goes to therapy now. That stuff is out of reach for me. She's got fancy health insurance, after all. And it's not like I'm neglected now.

I'm keeping food in the pantry. We pay our utilities. I do adult stuff like apply for agricultural grants to purchase my utility van for my bee business.

I am objectively okay.

Do I wish Eila had pushed for me to set up some hives here, for bees to help pollinate the native plants she's installing in the cemetery green spaces? Sure. But the job is new, and bees are a hard sell. Harder than goats. I get it.

It still stings.

I laugh out loud at my little joke, covering my mouth with my hand when I realize the crowd is listening to an un-funny history of the 1918 flu pandemic and how that changed the landscape of this historic cemetery. Yikes.

Eila was born for this work as a professional plant lady, and Esther opened a bar on purpose. Me? I never meant to become a beekeeper.

I happened to be in the right place one day when someone found bees in their garage and... I just knew what to do. I walked right up to them, found the queen, and waited for the others to follow.

Now, here I am, selling honey and beeswax salves and —when I'm really lucky—getting paid to remove bees from other people's property. I can charge whatever I want for that, and people pay. Nobody seems to understand these delicate creatures are so vital to our survival. The humans are just frightened. I'm glad they reach out to me before reaching for poison.

But today is about Eila. I'm happy for her and her sweetie, Ben. They're such opposites, but he's good for her, and she's so excited to move in with him. Even though I'm totally stuck with rent. Sure, I could move some place smaller and probably afford to live alone. But it's not just me.

I've got colonies of bees in the backyard, and that doesn't include the quarantine colonies I've stashed on Eila's lot next to our place. If I move out and someone moves in, it'll be weird and awkward for Eila and for me to go over there and deal with the hops and bees. It's better if I stay put. I'll figure something out about the rent.

The cemetery crowd moves to another part of the tour, and I walk along behind them. I clap politely as my sister proudly details the native plants. Who would have thought these old cemeteries were so carefully planned out? There's a flipping arboretum in here, and I just know those fruit trees would benefit from a nice, active colony of honeybees.

Eila slides her hands in her pockets, her attention flitting between the faces in the little crowd, and I wave from my place at the back. It's a pretty friendly bunch, consisting of all our sisters, their friends, and quite a few strangers here for the vibes. Should I have brought business cards? Is that slimy, to promote my work at my sister's shindig? My other sisters have a business promo baked in since they're participating.

My phone rings in my pocket. I back away from the group, hoping I'm not distracting Eila from her talk, and answer without glancing at the number. "Storm Swarm, this is Eden."

The caller coughs, and then I hear a voice I'd rather

forget. It goes with a face I'd rather forget, too—one I saw at the periphery of the wedding last week.

"Eden? Hey. I've got a problem."

I pull the phone away from my face and stare at it. I listed him in my contacts as *Actual Satan.*

"Eden? Are you there?" His voice sounds tinny, far away. I take a few breaths and turn my head over each shoulder, trying to decide if someone is pranking me.

"Nate?" I hate the way his name feels in my mouth, my tongue heavy with uncertainty. This guy screwed me over last year. Big time.

"Yeah. It's me. I was hoping—"

"If you're calling to report more diseases, I assure you I've had all the tests. You can jump in a river now. Bye."

"Eden, wait!" His voice is just desperate enough to halt my thumb before I press the red button to end the call. "I'm calling about a professional issue, I swear."

I frown. Today is Saturday, and it's late afternoon. Why is he working right now? Sounds fishy. "You have ninety seconds."

He sighs. "I'm flipping a house over in Morningside."

"So?" I wince, realizing he's barely more than a mile away from me at the moment.

"Well, um… the attic is full of bees."

My brows shoot up. "Oh yeah?"

"God, Eden, there must be a thousand of them. Inside the walls."

I laugh. "There are probably *eighty* thousand."

I listen to him exhale, trying not to remember the sound of him breathing near my ear while his clumsy hands roamed my body. "So, can you help me get rid of them? None of my guys will work with all that going on."

I look back at my sister, standing up on a rock and gesturing as she proudly describes responsible weed control here in the cemetery. I think again about the rent and the upcoming winter slow season. I need the money more than I need to avoid his stupid, smug face.

"It'll cost you," I hiss at Nate, before I spit out a fee double my usual rate to remove bees from a residential property.

"Fine. How soon can you be here?"

Shocked, I take a step backward and stumble. Composing myself, I mutter, "My stuff is in my van. Give me ten minutes."

Nate texts me an address, and I wave at Esther until she sees me. I point at my phone and mouth, "Work call."

She nods and gives me a thumbs up, and I head into the literal sunset to rescue my ex from a swarm of bees.

4

———

NATE

I AM INCREDIBLY UNCOMFORTABLE. Not only are there bees buzzing around the room, but a woman I've wronged is bent over, studying them, with her perfect ass in tight cut-off shorts, and I have absolutely no right to be memorizing the shape of it.

That night we spent together last year? I did a lot of that shit. I'm grateful she called me up to tell me about the STI. As far as I know, we both caught it early and cleared it up with meds. The whole thing was a wake-up call, though. I really should thank her.

And apologize.

I swat at a bee diving for my face as Eden peers into the tiny hole Chris smashed into the plaster before all hell broke loose. "Well?" I hope she can hear me above the racket. How did we miss all this last week when we were checking out the property?

I don't understand how Eden is just... bare handed, touching bees. She grunts. "You've got a colony in here.

These gals have been here for a minute. I bet the swarm at the church next door came from this group."

I swallow, and my mouth is chalky and dry. "So... what do we do?"

Eden stands up, hands on her hips. She's not even wearing one of those veils. "We?" She arches a brow, and I hold up my hands in surrender.

"You...? What do you do now? My guys are terrified and won't come near the property."

"That's a pretty typical response." Eden brushes a sweaty strand of hair from her face. "Can we talk options in another room? I don't want to disturb them at sunset."

I gesture toward the stairs, trying not to think about what times of day are bad manners to disturb a bunch of killer bees. Eden descends to the second floor and sits on the exposed hardwood. I squat across from her, not sure if it's safe to sit in case the bees come charging.

Eden brushes another strand of hair from her face, leaving a smear of dust on her cheek. My fingers twitch with the urge to wipe it clean.

"You know," she says, peering toward the attic, "I never thought I'd be here with you. Life's funny that way."

I swallow hard. "Yeah, funny. Listen, Eden, I really am sorry about—"

Eden presses her lips into a line. "I can get the queen out of the wall and relocate her. Maybe you saw the other day, but the bees will follow wherever she goes."

"Great. Do that. When will they be gone?"

She shakes her head. "That's just phase one. I'd have to open more of the wall to see, but I'm pretty certain you have a boatload of honey and beeswax in there."

I scratch my neck. "Define boatload."

Eden's face brightens and it's impossible to look away. "I'd guess there are multiple gallons of honey in there. And it'll be contained in the wax, so totally viable."

"Viable?"

"Yeah." She flaps a hand around. "To sell. Usually when I do hive management, there's no money exchanged. I split the honey fifty-fifty with the property owner, and I keep the wax."

"You keep the wax." I parrot her words like they make any sort of sense. She is approaching this professionally, though, so even though I'm turned on, I know I'm in good hands with this whole infestation.

Eden nods. "Yeah. I mean, I sell it, but I get all of it. I recommend we treat this as a hive management situation instead of a swarm removal. It'll mean you have to open the wall methodically. If we're careful, we can save the honey."

I scratch at the stubble I haven't gotten around to shaving. My father would tell me I look like a damn hipster. I stifle a surge of grief at the thought of him, and my ass finally finds the floor.

"I'll put a special device in the hole that will let the bees out but prevent them from returning," Eden continues. "As I said, I'll take the queen. Either way, you have to open the wall."

"Hmmmm." I frown. "You know I'm not the property owner, right? I'm just their contractor."

Eden's brows shoot up. "Okay... Call them, then. Tell

them my plan means no outlay of cash, plus a potential influx. And I can move the queen tonight." She looks toward the window. "If we move fast. I really don't want to dig in there after sunset. The bees will be doing night work. It's a whole thing."

I tell her to go ahead while I head outside to think. Much as I'd like to watch her dig a queen bee from a hole in the wall with her bare hands, I have a serious dilemma here. Eden's solution won't cost money, but she said it will take two weeks to deal with properly. We absolutely cannot sit on this project that long. But what other choice do I have?

By the time I see her walking out the door with another cardboard box full of bees and a smile on her face, I've already decided not to tell the owner. Eden sets the bees on the ground and turns toward me, skin nearly glowing under the streetlight, eyes sparkling with joy and satisfaction. She's so competent, and I had no idea it would turn me on to watch a woman charm bees, but here I am, half hard despite a stress headache.

I follow her to the curb and cough. "Do you, uh, need me to do anything? With the plug thingy?"

Hollow amusement fills her tone. "I think you've done enough."

I blow out a breath. "God, Eden, I'm so sorry about how things went down last year."

Her head tilts back, brow furrowed. "How things *went down?*"

"I'm sorry I got plastered and gave you a disease. It's not an excuse or anything, but the explanation is that my dad had just died, and I was—"

Her face softens. "I didn't know that. About your father."

"Heart attack." I lean against her van, the metal warm from the day's heat. "Dead before he hit the ground."

She winces. "That's so awful, Nate." Eden stiffens and rolls her lips between her teeth. "I wish I knew this a year ago." She opens the back of her van and shoves the bees inside, turning to face me before shutting the door. "I should have probably been more assertive about using a condom."

I let my head fall against the side of the van. "Aw hell, we didn't even use a condom?"

Eden lifts a shoulder. "I guess we were both reckless. Making bad decisions all around."

I humph in agreement. "Lucky nothing worse happened."

"Worse than gonorrhea?"

My eyes fly wide. "Yeah. Like something incurable? Or, you know..." I don't finish the sentence because there's really no decent way to say I'm glad I didn't knock up a total stranger when I was drunk and deep in grief. "I have my shit together a little more now. I go to a group. At the church, actually. That's how I learned about this hot property." I gesture at the sagging porch and overgrown lawn.

Eden laughs. That's got to be something, right? A laugh? She seems to gather her composure and backs toward the driver's seat door without breaking eye contact. "I appreciate your apology, Nate. And the context."

She climbs into the driver's seat. "Hey," I blurt. "What happens next? With the bees?"

Eden taps her chin, considering. "I'll have to get supplies. We should give them a few days to fully vacate. So meet me here Tuesday?"

She tells me to hang plastic at the entrance to the third floor and the guys can work on the other floors of the house. And then she drives off with a van full of bees, which is how I feel inside knowing I'm going to be working closely with this woman. Maybe by the time we finish the project, I'll have figured out a way to get her to forgive me.

5

EDEN

MONDAY FAMILY DINNER is sacrosanct for the Storm girls. Esther's bar is closed, and family dinner is pretty much the only time she ever sits down. Eila and I are hosting one last time as roommates, but it's been too hot to cook, so we're eating a giant salad she put together from all her many plants. My big contribution is honey dressing. Of course.

I set the cute little pitcher on the table just in time for Eila to announce, "Eden's been hanging out with Disease Dick again."

I freeze, a flush creeping through my cheeks that's unrelated to the humidity and heavy heat. "Eila, God. What a way to phrase it."

She points at me with the salad tongs. "Did he or did he not give you the clap last year? With his penis?" She sways the tongs back and forth. "A diseased... dick..."

Eva chortles, and Eliza arches a brow. I have to set the record straight. "Look, he didn't *know* he had it. And I was making bad choices that night, too."

Esther's husband, Koa, shakes his head. "Why are you seeing this fella?"

Esther points at me with her fork. "You always wrap it, Eden. I've been over this."

I roll my eyes and sink onto the wobbly stool I dragged in from the living room to complete our eclectic seating. It's nice expanding our table to include Ben and Koa. It reminds me of a TV family, and TV families always make room for more. "Nate's a client now. His construction site has a colony of bees inside a wall."

Eliza takes a bite of her salad, chewing noisily. "Will you quarantine the shit out of the bees in case they have extra diseases?"

Eva snorts, and Ben groans, like he never wants to discuss a penis ever again. At least not with his girlfriend's family. I cross my arms defensively, although I'm not at all sure why I feel defensive of Nate Donovan. "If you must know, he apologized. His dad died suddenly, and he was in a dark place, and he sees some sort of grief counselor now. And I am getting more out of the deal. I negotiated keeping half the honey from inside the wall."

"Hmm." Esther furrows her brow and turns to Koa. Koa lost both his parents, but as far as I know, he didn't resort to self-destruction. He did marry my sister after knowing her for an hour, but that was less impulsive and more practical—he needed a green card.

"So anyway," I try to change the subject. "The wall project is really interesting to me. I am using a bee escape tool I had to customize since there were some other holes in the wall. I got the majority of the bees out already, but—"

"Are you sure you have the capacity for this project?" Esther doesn't usually interrupt me, so I'm really rattled when she leans across the table and pats my arm. "I want to make sure you're expanding intentionally, slowly. Trust me when I say it's not easy having more work than you can handle."

I scrunch my face. "Thanks? And it's not a lot of hands-on work at this point." I'm not sure why my sister is being so bossy, especially when she knows I'm up a creek about rent.

Okay, yes, I've cried to her on the phone a few times when I had way too much honey to process at once and had to beg my sisters to help me get it into jars. But I have a different business model now—selling the honey by the bucketful. Hopefully, the two new colonies I gained this week will really amp up my honey production and the income from selling it.

And what does Esther know about me expanding too rapidly? I absolutely need as much income as I can get. For starters, I'm using vintage, inefficient equipment I got at an estate sale. I glance over at Ben, who works as an inspector for the city, and remember I never got around to filing the permit paperwork to keep hives here at the rental property. Shit.

I'm about to change the subject again, when there's a knock at the door. "Girls? Yoohoo!" It's a voice I haven't heard in a few months, and it sends my heart into a deep freeze.

Our mother.

Esther's face tightens. Eliza looks like she's going to vomit. Eila claps a hand over her mouth. "How did she find us?" she hisses, running fingers through her hair to straighten it, like she knows our mother is about to lecture her appearance.

Eva slouches low in her seat and bites her lip. "So, um, you know how I have Esther's old phone?" She explains Mom called looking for Esther and, Eva being Eva, now we have another guest for dinner. "I didn't think she'd actually show up."

"Oh, Christ." Esther throws her napkin on the table and stomps toward the front door, Eliza hot on her heels. "Emma Storm, what are you doing here?"

"Esther!" Mom rushes in and hugs Esther like it's been a week since she saw us. "So good to see you, sweetheart." She wraps her arms around my stiff sister as we peer around the wall. Mom takes in the room. "Oh, you're all here. This is so wonderful. And there's food!"

Mom darts around the room, planting wet kisses on our cheeks. She doesn't seem to notice the men until she lowers into Esther's seat and peers up at Esther's huge, muscular husband. "Well, well... Who are *you* and can I get your number?"

Koa frowns. "My wife was sitting there."

Mom looks at the chair, avoiding the word *wife*. "One of my girls? Well, she can give her old mom a seat and find her own." Mom glances around again. "This place is so... creative."

Eila and I painted each room a different color, both because we love bright colors and because it hides the stains. We love living in a crayon box.

Esther leans against a teal wall, arms folded in a

defensive posture. Koa rises to join her, planting a kiss on her cheek. "Shall I get the car, love?"

Esther shakes her head, and he stands by her side like a shield. I wonder briefly if he'd shield the rest of us, too.

Eliza—who never got a hug and seems to prefer it that way—asks, "What are you doing here?"

Mom takes a sip of Esther's water. "Oh, I have the best news. I have a lead on a real opportunity here in Pittsburgh. I'm back, girls. For good."

None of us say anything, and Mom seems to wait for us to cheer and pop champagne. She circles a finger in the air. "I just need a place to hang for a few days while I talk to my partners. Whose house was this again, Eva? You've got room for your mommy, right?"

Esther glares at our baby sister, who makes a face like she's constipated. "This is Eden and Eila's house, and they only have two bedrooms."

Ben, who is autistic and struggles to let things go when they're not precisely accurate, blurts, "Eila moved in with me, so her room is free. She even left her bed—ow!"

Eila elbows him in the neck. Normally, we'd probably defend Ben and yell at our sister for being a dick, but he blew our excuse.

"Oh," Mom coos. "That sounds like my timing was perfect. Eden, it'll be me and you! Like old times. Who can get my things from the curb? The Lyft driver wouldn't stick around while I asked for help getting them up all those rickety stairs. Don't worry—I won't be leaving a tip."

I study all my sisters, at Ben and Koa. Everyone seems as uncomfortable as I feel. Frankly, I'd rather sleep in Eliza's goat shed than stay here with the woman who left for days at a time if her boyfriend of the hour wanted her at his side for a trip. I was changing my sisters' diapers when I was barely out of them myself, and I don't want to clean any more Emma Storm-related messes.

But I also don't want to toss my mother to the curb with her bags. I never want to be that inconsiderate, even though Mom never did much to help us in the past. "I'll grab your stuff, Mom."

"No, no, I got it." Eva rushes to the door, and I let her, since apparently, she got us into this mess. It's hard to fault her, when I'm doing just as much enabling.

I take a deep breath. "Let me show you around the house." I hear my sisters cleaning the dishes while I walk Mom past the half-bath, living room, and toward the stairs.

Mom runs her finger along the arm of my favorite thrift chair in the living room. Mom has dyed her hair onyx black. I swear she had laugh lines and wrinkles the last time I saw her, but now her skin is strangely smooth and stiff. I wonder how she afforded to get this sort of work done, thinking about what she would have traded for vanity.

Mom frowns at the room and says, "I didn't realize 'mismatched' was a style choice. You've certainly committed to it, haven't you?"

The comment stings, reminding me that Mom always cares about appearances, but not enough to take responsibility for how things appear. I respond with a "hm," and gesture toward the stairs. Mom walks up and stops at my room.

"Oh, Eden, you know men prefer a clean, welcoming space. You're not going to land a husband with a sloppy room like this."

My room has been cleaner, sure. Laundry is piled up because I spent my weekend dealing with Eila's event and Nate's wall. I should correct her. I should tell her I don't base my decorating and housekeeping decisions on what a man might think. But she's moved on to the other room, muttering about color choices and the *character* of the house.

I nudge Mom toward the back set of stairs, which leads to the mudroom where I keep all my beekeeping gear. Mom reaches out to touch the vintage honey extractor, and I snap. "Don't touch that."

Mom's eyes widen like I slapped her face. I don't think I've ever spoken sharply to her before, but I rely on that extractor to keep this eclectic roof over my head. "It's for my work. You can't touch my work stuff, okay? You must not, under any circumstances, open the freezer or touch its contents."

After the last tearful honey bottling, I've taken to processing in batches, and I have the frames in the deep freeze until I can get to them. I'm waiting for a shipment of new containers, so it's been a minute, and the freezer is full.

"Eden, baby, I would never touch your things. You know me." Mom appears hurt at the suggestion. I'm probably a minute away from loudly accepting her apology and hugging her, but my phone rings.

I pull it from my pocket, and for the first time, I'm grateful when I see Nate's name on my caller ID.

"I have to take this," I call to the entire household, not pausing to consider how quickly I shifted to gratitude at the sight of Nate's name.

6

NATE

I KNOW Eden told me to wait until Tuesday, but I couldn't help myself. I go up to the third floor at the Morningside house. I scream like a child when I see the honey oozing out and around Eden's plug device. A bunch of bees fly around the place, super confused.

I almost wish they'd sting my eyes. I'd rather deal with that than have to call Kenneth in Manhattan—or whatever his name is—and tell him his investment property is oozing and infested.

Instead, I panic and call Eden. She seems eager to check things out, so maybe my curiosity paid off?

Eden's van slows outside, and I watch as she parallel parks, fitting into a space I wouldn't have even attempted. She's always so quietly excellent at everything.

She climbs out of the van all business, and my words fall away. I want to thank her for coming in the evening. I want to compliment her parking job. Instead, I gawk like a fool.

She approaches, smelling like honey and flowery shampoo. And maybe a little sweat. I like it.

"Hey," she says. "You mentioned a situation?"

"Oh." I scratch my head like the bumbling idiot I've become. "Yeah. I think you should take a look."

Eden tucks her bee veil under one arm.

I point at it. "How do you decide when to wear that thing?"

She smiles, like I've asked her the best question. I like knowing I said the right thing. "Bees are particular this time of day. They're trying to get back to their home, maybe stressing out about the pollen haul. I try to be extra careful if I think the wee folk will get jumpy."

"So *just a veil* is you being extra careful? If I see you in the full suit, I should run, right?"

She laughs and nods. "Show me this mess."

I guide her toward the house and through the plastic curtain I taped up to block the third floor. The guys and I got a lot of demo done today, so we both have to climb around a bunch of debris to get there.

"What did the owner say about splitting the honey?" She glances over her shoulder, dark eyes and dark hair illuminated by the orange glow of the sunset through the windows.

"God, you're gorgeous."

A wobbly laugh falls from Eden's lips. "I doubt that's what they said."

I wince. "Sorry. I just..." I shrug. "Look, I didn't tell the owner. He doesn't live in this state. All he cares about is meeting the deadline under budget. I don't even want the honey. You should take all of it and promise not to tell anyone where you got it." I blow a raspberry. "Now you know my deep, unprofessional secret."

She frowns. "Am I going to get cited for trespassing? Like, does the guy even know I'm here?" Her tone is harsher than I've ever heard from her, and my brows shoot toward my hairline. I watch as Eden regains her composure. "Sorry. Sorry. I don't want to lose my temper with you. Are you sure this is above board?"

I shift my weight from foot to foot. "Hey, I get it. I promise nobody is going to say anything about you taking honey from this property." I feel confident in this assertion; there's no universe where Kenneth The Jagoff will show up before Eden empties out this wall.

Eden purses her lips. "Well, I just remembered I never filed the permit paperwork to have my beehives at my house, so now you know my deep, unprofessional secret, too."

We smile at each other for a beat until she turns and continues up the stairs, giving me a terrific view of her toned legs and muscular calves above the work boots and slouched socks she wears with her shorts.

Eden peers into the sting-room. "Hey, girls. You lost?"

I stay behind in the doorway and watch as she rips the plastic off one of the windows. A few seconds later, the remaining bees fly out the window into the darkening sky.

"I should have thought of that," I confess. "But you said to limit their access."

"They would have found a way out eventually. They're searching for the queen. Gosh, I hope they didn't incubate a new one in there since I left." Eden scurries to the hole in the wall, prying off her device and peering inside. "Do you have a flashlight?"

I step toward her, pulling the pen light from one of my pockets and handing it over, loving the warm connection when my fingers touch her palm. She clicks on the light and presses her face into the hole in the wall, ignoring the honey mess. "Whew," she says, handing me the light. "Doesn't seem like there's much activity. I think the honey seepage is from the heat."

I take the pen light from her hand, swallowing. Eden taps her bee plug into place. It's the size of one of Sparky's palms, with a tube-like protrusion, and Eden uses a little beeswax to hold it in place. "I think I should get started on this wall before any more of the wax melts. Tomorrow?"

"Okay." My words come slowly. I'm so distracted by how beautiful she is, how calmly she's handling this unexpected construction snafu. How badly I want to try again to be with her. I think I stun both of us when I blurt out, "I'd like to take you on a date after all this."

Eden blinks. She sags against the wall, not caring that it's dirty and sticky and... God, I need to not think about a dirty, sticky Eden and how she'll get clean.

"Nate," she whispers, shaking her head. "I need this to be professional. This is my job."

Heat rushes through my neck and behind my ears. "Of course. I'm sorry. I had no business asking."

Eden seems like she wants to talk about it, though. She twirls some brown hair around a finger and her shoulders lower. "My mom just showed up out of freaking nowhere. And my sister is moving out. Honestly,

I'm really glad you're letting me have the honey, because I need the money. Ugh, I'm rambl—Oh!"

I step back, giving her space, not sure what made her exclaim this time. I search for a spider or stray bee or something.

She reaches for her phone. "I should call Dr. Shultz about the wall. She's my mentor. Sort of."

"Mentor?"

Eden nods. "I did take classes at the college extension program. But most of what I know I learned from Marsha Shultz. She will know if the colony is fully gone, and we can move ahead with the harvest. She's been urging me to make weed honey for higher profit margins. Honestly, I think I will try a CBD salve with the beeswax." Eden glances at her phone. "I'm rambling again, aren't I?"

"I don't mind." And it's true. The guys on my crew are men of few words, and apart from the hour a week I visit the grief group, I don't really get to talk to anyone. Until Eden started talking about her mentor, I didn't even realize how much I missed just hearing people yack. My dad was a talker. He used to recap our days over dinner at our house, like I didn't spend the whole time with him and live it all myself. My brows raise almost to my hairline. I am utterly charmed by this word vomit.

Eden blows out a breath. "Well... Marsha sells her stuff by word-of-mouth. It's just a side hustle for her. I'd like to sell in bulk to, like, restaurants, you know? And find a consignment arrangement for the cosmetic stuff. I'm not cut out for weekly markets."

"I can see where a wholesale model would be easier,"

I add, proud I could pull the word *wholesale* from my muddled mind.

Eden hums in agreement and heads toward the stairs. "I'm going to see if Marsha can meet me here in the morning before she goes to work. Be ready—she's a talker."

"'Cause you're the silent type?" I hope it's okay to tease her, and I'm relieved when Eden smiles—a real, all-the-way-to-her-eyes grin I can just make out from the streetlight through the front windows.

"See you in the morning." She climbs into her van, and when she's out of sight, I sink to the curb, elbows on my knees and head in my hands. I've always had a sweet tooth, and I'm starting to crave Eden Storm.

7

NATE

Eden's friend Marsha is... a whole lot. She showed up on a motorcycle, chrome glinting in the morning sun, and strode right in like she owned the place. I wish she was the owner. She seems like she'd be better to work with than some out-of-state guy who never emails complete sentences.

"You the guy to see?" she asks as I fumble with my clipboard. The guys start the bandsaw just as I open my mouth to tell her about the situation. Eden isn't here yet. It all feels foreboding.

I swallow and hold out a hand, which she grips in a firm shake. "I'm Nate Donovan. Eden is... oh, there she is." Relief floods my system at the sight of her, fresh and fragrant with her hair spilling everywhere, wearing just a tank top and those damn tiny cut-offs. She doesn't have a veil with her today. Marsha catches me staring and gives me a look. I fake a cough behind my fist and try to regroup.

"Marsh!" Eden throws her arms around her mentor,

and I'm a little surprised to see the good doctor embrace Eden warmly. Marsha snaps right back into business mode upon release and pulls a pair of coveralls from her bag.

Marsha steps into the heavy garment, shaking her head in Eden's direction. "I still think you're nuts going in there like that. A bee flew up my nose yesterday. That was with the veil on."

"They like me." Eden shrugs. "I don't know how to explain it."

I almost say that everyone likes her. I should say *something*—offer Eden and her friend... what exactly? I can't pull an espresso out of my rear end. I only have electricity because we've got a generator going.

Marsha frowns with her whole body, scolding Eden from inside her veil. "You don't have smoke with you?"

Eden shakes her head. "They're mostly gone. I'm sure they hated leaving their brood behind..."

The two of them chatter about best practices in these cases, and I can tell they care more about the bees than the structural integrity of the house.

By the time I make it to the third floor behind them, they're both crouched next to the hole in the wall, murmuring quietly. I stand back and watch Eden in her element, explaining how she put the exit-only tunnel on the wall outside the hive. Marsha acknowledges it would have been difficult to save the babies, and Eden's relief is apparent even to me. I hadn't realized there were babies in the wall.

"Whelp." Marsha flicks a few bees from her legs with

a gloved hand. "I'd say you're on the right track. We still on for tonight?"

Eden nods and I focus on the hem of her tank top, a little damp with sweat I want to taste. She fans herself and I wish she'd step closer so I could fan her myself.

Marsha sniffs and catches me ogling Eden. "Oof. The hetero hormones here are getting too much for me," Marsha says, giving me a salute. She spins on her heel and takes off down the stairs. Eden sends me a *look*. It's more than a body scan. It's a hot look, suggesting I'm not alone in my struggle to hold myself together. But I have to let Eden take the lead on whatever she has in mind behind that glance. I'm the one in atonement mode, and Eden quickly reverts to professionalism.

I can just hear the roar of Marsha's motorcycle above the saws and generators downstairs, and maybe I stand extra close to Eden. She can hear me better... yeah, that's the reason. "What did she say?"

Eden plucks her plug from the wall with a smile. "The grownup bees have moved out. We will need to pull the plaster off in small bits, methodically, so we can see where the honeycomb is attached. We are good to go if you've got a crowbar or something."

I pull a power drill from my belt and rev the motor a few times. "Oh, I'm ready," I joke. I switch the head of the drill to my saw attachment kit, and Eden watches, intrigued, head tilted as if she is studying my movements as I cut through the plaster as shallowly as possible. A house this old wouldn't have insulation, so there's just a gap between the plaster and the framing. Some dusty chunks crack off and fall to the floor, revealing...

"What the hell is that?"

"Ooooh," Eden coos, leaning in. She points at a white, lumpy substance that looks like mold and tells me it's capped honeycomb. "Each of those slabs will have a few pounds of honey inside. The white caps keep it nice and sanitary. Hang on, I have to run to my van and grab something." She pushes to her feet, narrowing her eyes and pointing a disciplining finger at me. "Touch. Nothing."

As if I would reach in there. I search for signs of life in the wall and find none. Soon Eden clomps back up the steps, dragging a giant blue cooler in one hand and carrying a black bucket in the other. She's got a mini crowbar-looking tool sticking out the waist of her tiny shorts. I imagine how much easier her work would be with a tool belt, and then I can't stop picturing her in a tool belt.

I clear my throat. "Tell me what to do."

"Well, big guy, we're going to very gently pry the comb from the studs." Eden coughs and pats her chest. Her cheeks go red and I swallow, fighting a grin.

She shows me how to jimmy the honeycomb loose from the wall, and we get to work peeling it from the joists.

"Where will you put all this?" There's so much from those little buzzers.

"Hmm..." Eden taps her chin. "I guess I need to get food-grade buckets or gallon jars if I'm going to do wholesale, huh?"

I shrug. "I'm the wrong guy to ask."

She sighs. "I'm so bad at all those little details. Like, who knows what containers to order? Not me."

"I feel you on that. Apparently, I'm supposed to be ordering all the rulers and pencils and extra sandpaper for this operation. Did I do that? Nope."

We trade growing pain stories—her with her micro-farm, me with my father's microbusiness. She hums. "I know it's probably nothing to file the right paperwork and get more grant funding. But even the letters USDA sound intimidating." Eden turns to face me, eyes huge, arms full of honeycomb. "Is that dumb?"

"Not at all." This woman gets me. She is so obviously good at what she does, and yet so stymied by the little things. She makes a few trips to her van for more coolers and buckets until I imagine we have the entire Yeti product line full of honeycomb.

Eden assesses her armful of comb, puts the good ones in the cooler to "process," and tells me to toss the bad ones in her bucket. "I'll melt all that and set it near my hives. My other bees will salvage almost all of this."

"You running a scrapyard?" I heave a piece of comb from the wall. It's almost as tall as Eden, and she giggles as I try to put it in the cooler.

"You'll have to cut that one in half. Gently."

I glance around. She only has one of those flat tools, so I'm not sure how she wants me to proceed. The flat-head screwdriver from my own tool belt hasn't been nearly as effective. I eventually shrug and snap the comb in half. I'm rewarded with two palms full of warm honey.

"Do you have a rubber band?" Eden whips her head around as she asks, accidentally bumping my hand into my face. "Oh. Nate, I'm sorry." I touch my cheek, a goopy drop dribbling down my skin.

Eden looks flustered. Her chest rises and falls rapidly and I can see her pulse jump at her throat. "Here, let me."

My own heart skips when Eden absently wipes honey from near my lip. My entire body is aware of her touch, until she pauses with her thumb on my cheek. I'm very, very glad I shaved this morning as Eden presses the pad of her thumb against my skin, wiping away the warm honey. And then, she puts her thumb into her mouth and sucks it clean.

I see the moment she realizes what she's doing. Her eyes fly wide in a blend of horror and embarrassment. Before I can reach for her or tell her she's very welcome to lick honey off any part of my body, she emits a tiny yip and runs out of the house, dragging the cooler behind her.

8

———

EDEN

"You just ran away?" Eva stares at me, wide-eyed, in my kitchen, where I'm draped over a stool.

I drag my hands down my face with a groan, glad I could call my sister in my hour of need.

Eva pours herself the last of the coffee and adds ice from the tray in the freezer. She leans against the counter. "So, you talked about bees, you filled coolers and buckets with bee gunk, and—"

"It's honeycomb. And propolis. We've been through this." I glance through my fingers at my sister's irritated scowl and wince.

"Anyway... You filled these coolers, he got some honey on his face, you licked him, and you ran away?"

I don't know what came over me. Heat stroke? Delayed inebriation? I turned around and Nate Donovan looked unbelievably sexy in his tight t-shirt and that fucking toolbelt, and he had honey on his face. "I licked my *thumb...* but I was making eyes."

"Hmm." She slurps her iced coffee. "I don't get it, though. Why run away? You already boned."

I shake my head. "Do you remember Eila driving me to urgent care afterward when I got a fever and had weird discharge?" Eva snorts. I growl. "I yelled at him a lot after that. Well, his voicemail. But now he's my client, and it's inappropriate for me to lick anything or think about him that way."

Eva crunches the ice from her coffee. "And?"

I flail my hands around. "And he seems kind of vulnerable and hotly responsible now, but who even knows if that was a sham? Like which Nate is the real one, you know?"

I'm spared having to sort through any more of my feelings about Nate because my mother breezes into the room in what I believe to be Esther's bathrobe. "Morning, roomie! Oh, dear. You didn't make coffee?"

Mom frowns at the empty coffeemaker on the counter and mugs resting in the sink. I don't have an opportunity to defend myself—and I swear I would—because Mom snaps her attention to Eva. "Baby daughter! Come give your mama a hug." Mom pats Eva on the back stiffly, like she doesn't quite know how hugs work. "What brings you by our humble abode today?" I don't miss how Mom emphasizes the word *humble*.

She flits toward me, taking a seat expectantly, and I realize she's waiting to be served coffee. Should I make more?

"Did I hear you mention something about being mean to a man, Eden darling?" she asks. "You know that's no way to get one to stick around."

Sometimes I think the things my mother says have to be a test. Like she can't really believe she's an expert on getting men to stick around when she had five daughters from four different members of the test pool.

Eva attempts to defend me. "Eden was telling me about an ex who she now has to see at work."

"At your bee work? I still can't believe that's a real job. You'll have to show me. I mean, I can plant flowers! Why have I been busting my bum on the casino circuit when I could be a bee lady?"

I tap my fingers on my lap. "You might be a natural at it. Maybe I got it from you."

Mom nods enthusiastically. "Yes, this is the ticket. Roomies. Business partners. What will you do today when you start work?"

I glance at the clock. "Um, this has been my lunch break."

Seeing and smelling no food in the kitchen, Mom frowns and stands back up. "Give me five minutes to change, and you can put me to work. I'll earn my keep, right? Always do."

Eva makes a face as Mom skips upstairs, perhaps to change. Maybe to read a magazine and wait for someone to cook her a meal.

I grunt and turn to my sister. "Thank you for bringing me a sandwich and listening to my horror story."

Evie cringes. "It's literally the least I can do after I dumped Mom on you."

I wave a hand. "It could have happened to any of us. None of us are any good at setting boundaries with her."

"Esther is." Eva grabs her purse and pats her pockets

for her phone. "I'll take her car to her and ask for lessons in boundary setting."

"Love you," I call after her.

When she's gone, I drag the cooler into the mudroom toward the chest freezer. At least I had the sense to grab the cooler when I ran from Nate. It's not a terribly big deal that I left the bucket. I was going to melt all that stuff anyway. I really ought to go back and keep pulling honeycomb from the wall, but I don't think I can see Nate at least for another hundred years or so.

By the time I'm ready to go outside and check on the two colonies of quarantined bees, Mom shocks the hell out of me by showing up in the kitchen in jeans, a long-sleeved shirt, and decent shoes. "I'm ready," she says. "Fly me to the bees!" She snorts. "It's a Sinatra joke. Get it?"

I humor her with a smile and gesture toward the yard. "The hives along the hillside are my permanent bees. There are a bunch of colonies there, but they should be in good shape. Today we need to check on the new girls." I point toward the temporary hives by the front left edge of the property, near Eila's hops crop. Bees buzz happily among the late-season cones. Hops are wind-pollinated, but the oils on the plants themselves help protect bees from mites.

Mom practically skips to the boxes. "It smells so good. Are those your sister's plants? What are they?" Mom smooshes her face into a hops cone and inhales. I bite my lip, fighting my urge to answer every one of her questions, because all us Storm girls agreed we can't have Mom interfering with anything we rely on for income.

It's one thing for me to give her a tour of the yard with

my bees. But I know I shouldn't risk Mom damaging Eila's microfarm project. She's got contracts with local breweries depending on this crop of hers.

It's hard for me to draw hard lines with Mom. She isn't some evil villain. She has her moments, like when I turned ten and she surprised us with tickets to Kennywood. Mom rode the carousel with us, held our backpacks while we rode the bumper cars, and even convinced Esther to put her arms up on the Thunderbolt.

"Why don't we check on the new bees?" I say, holding out a veil for my mother.

"Don't you need one of these?"

I shake my head. "The bees are calm today."

Mom drops the veil in the grass. "If you don't need it, then I'm good, too. You must have gotten your bee-charming from me, right?"

I suppress a groan. "I'm going to open the lid and make sure everyone is healthy. If there are no signs of disease and if everyone is working on a new brood comb, I'll build another permanent hive for this crew."

I pull my hive tool from my shorts pocket and lift the lid. "Hey, girls," I whisper. "I'm just checking in. Everyone doing okay in here? Oh, look!" I press a hand to my chest. "Mom, they're making so many baby bees already."

I'll never know what Mom thinks of baby bees, because as soon as I invite her to see them, she starts screaming. "It's in my hair!"

"Mom, you need to step away from the—do *not* do that."

Mom kicks her legs. "They're crawling up my pants! I

can feel them!" Mom flaps her arms. I try to guide her to the road, away from the bees. But I'm too late.

With a thud, Mom kicks over the temporary cardboard hive. The bees burst free, scattering. I've never actually seen this sort of bee behavior, and I reach for the discarded bee veil in the grass since I'm not sure how they'll act. I quietly panic, wondering if I should chase my mother down the street where she took off, or if I should try to save the colony.

Mom seems to have found a neighbor to share in her horror. I can see them gesturing and pointing, and I hear them both yelling about "murder hornets." I sigh and squat next to the box, trying to pick it up. I search among the cracked and bent bits of honeycomb, looking for the queen. My heart sinks as I see that she's gone. She left the babies behind, again, and fled with her swarm of attendants.

This whole disaster reeks of massive failure, an inexplicable loss, and I nearly choke when I hear the chirp of a police cruiser. It pulls over by Mom and the neighbor— is that Ms. Grishom? Did they really call the police about bees?

I'm dejectedly plucking honeycomb from the asphalt when a shadow settles over me, and my stomach sinks. My bee permit isn't exactly kosher at the moment. These poor bees. Will I have to get rid of them? Will they spray them? Not everyone gets the importance of their existence.

I try taking a deep breath, choking a bit on the wetness in my throat. I sniff away the tears, but it's no use. I'm a puffy red mess, I'm sure of it.

The shadow moves, and a bandana wiggles next to my ear, the scent of sawdust reaching my nostrils.

I whip around, my wet eyes drifting up a pair of dirty jeans, a toolbelt, white tee, to the calming, sympathetic smile of the man I least expected to be here.

"Need a hand?"

9

NATE

"How did you know?" Eden asks, her lashes wet. She reaches for my offered bandana and dabs at her cheeks.

"How did I know you needed help?" A blend of emotions wrestles in my chest at the sight of Eden weeping amidst the chaos of a kicked over beehive. "For starters, you ran out of my house like it was on fire. You left your bucket of... What did you call this stuff again?"

Eden sniffles and removes the veil. "It's dirty honeycomb. Just like all this." She gestures at the oozing heap, honey glistening on the toe of her boot.

I hear the crunch of shoes on gravel and look up to see a pair of police officers approaching. Farther down the street, a pair of women clings to the wall of a house, staring intently at the cops. I hope they don't want to watch Eden get hauled away. There's no way I'm letting that happen.

"Can we help you?" I straighten to my full height, hooking my thumbs in my belt loops. Eden's lip trembles.

One of the officers swats at an errant bee. "Ma'am, we had a call that you unleashed a swarm of killer bees…"

"Let me stop you right there," I interject. "Eden keeps honeybees. They're a protected species. She's working with the USDA, and she is not the one who kicked this hive and set them loose."

Eden's eyes widen with every word I utter, like she's never had anyone defend her before. *Well, get used to it, sugar. I'm sweet on you.*

The older police officer works a piece of gum and furrows his brow. "Are you the property owner?"

I shake my head. Eden blurts, "I rent. I haven't seen my landlord in years."

The younger cop scratches the back of his neck. The street is peaceful and calm. The bees from Eden's quarantine hive—are they the ones that were in the wall?—are long gone, for the most part. "Do you have the necessary paperwork to keep bees here?"

"What bees?" I ask, pointing to Eden's feet. "All I see is an empty box spilling some honey. You gonna cite her for littering?"

"All right, now," the older cop says, turning to the younger cop. "I don't even know how we'd write this one up." He hooks a thumb in my direction. "Big guy here is right. The bees are gone, as best I can tell."

I wince, spotting the brightly colored hives in Eden's backyard, hoping he doesn't look too closely.

He doesn't. He continues talking to his partner. "What do you think? Domestic disturbance, all clear on arrival?"

The younger officer takes a step back, his heel sinking into a fresh stream of honey oozing from the toppled box.

He makes a face and wipes his heel in the grass. "Yeah, sounds good." He gives Eden a small smile. "Take care, now."

With that, they make their way to their cruiser, not engaging with the women on the stoop. Eden glares down the road and mumbles, "Don't worry about it, Mom. I'll clean up."

I frown. "That's your mom?"

Her eyes well up and her gaze drops to the ground. "That was Emma Storm doing what she does."

"What's that? Stir shit?" When Eden doesn't respond, I bite back a growl as I drape an arm around her shoulders. "Should I get the hose?"

She shakes her head. "That will be the last step. Let's see what we can salvage."

I help her carry the detritus to her house and sort through it, adding more bits to the black bucket I brought. I marvel at how carefully she saves rubber bands, wipes down wooden frames, and mends the cardboard.

"You don't waste anything, do you?"

She glances at her work. "I guess not. I grew up knowing there might not be more of anything." She shrugs. "Hard habit to break. Plus the bees are really resourceful."

I smile at her enthusiasm. "I wish I could salvage more in my work. I have a ton of smaller bits of wood in my dad's—in my shed."

The corner of her mouth twitches. "Will you tell me about him?" I nod and she gestures toward the house, walking toward the shade.

I sink to the step on the back porch. "Well, he smoked too much. Regrets that now, I suppose."

She blinks at my black humor and I forget I'm not at grief group where everyone makes these kinds of jokes. Eden coughs. "Come on, Nate. That's not what I meant."

I squint at the bright garden, at the painted row of beehives. "He was always there for me. Dependable as the sun, he used to say." I shift my focus to my shoelaces. "Mom didn't stick around long. I guess I was a fussy baby. They were never married."

Eden sits next to me on the stoop. "Babies are like that, I hear. Fussy."

"He liked routine." I think about my dad making the same meals on the same days of the week for decades. Always spaghetti on Monday, tacos on Tuesday, quesadillas on Wednesday. The man assembled ten sandwiches every Sunday evening and had me wiping off apples to line up for our lunches. "He was organized, but he didn't write anything down. Nothing I've been able to find, at any rate. I think he stored it all upstairs." I tap the side of my head and sigh. "Honestly, I have no clue what I'm doing. It's been an entire year, and I feel like I'm on the verge of being discovered as a huge fraud."

"Fraud... that's a familiar word." Eden glances down the road; there's no sign of Emma or the neighbor. "I think I'm just going through the motions with my business. I know I'm good at the bee part. But there's so much paperwork and rules, and I almost died when you told the police about me and the USDA because I swear, Nate, if they ever check to see what I did with that grant money, they'll suck it all back."

I laugh. "I don't think it works like that. Money's long spent, right?"

"You never know." She shakes her head. "Can I confess something awful?"

"Hit me."

Eden wrinkles her nose and takes a deep breath. "I was really jealous there, when you were talking about your dad. Being organized... being there at all. I never had that. I think mine and Eila's dad lives here in Pittsburgh, but we sure never hear from him. And Mom is..." Eden gestures.

"What's her deal?" I lean forward, clasping my hands. My thigh is pressed against Eden's, and the heat from her leg burns through my jeans.

"My sister Esther says it's the patriarchy. Like Mom was sort of raised to believe her only worth was in keeping a man around, so she devoted everything to making men happy. Then she'd have to start over when they'd inevitably leave."

"And she wasn't organized? How many Storms are there?"

Eden laughs. "Five of us. All girls. Four different fathers. Esther was really the one who raised us. The second she had a house big enough, she took us from Mom's apartment, and honestly, I'm not sure my mother noticed for a few months. She was in her pyramid scheme era, traveling to Vegas for workshops on how to sell better chamois towels or knives or whatever."

"Maybe she took my mom with her."

"Yeah." Eden leans on her elbows and closes her eyes, turning her face toward the sun. "Maybe."

I hear the crunch of shoes on gravel. Speak of the devil. Eden's mother moves in front of us, blocking the sun from our eyes. "I assume you've shooed away all the creatures?"

Eden opens her eyes. I expect her to yell; the woman cost her a colony of bees, but she sort of shrinks into herself, and her lip wobbles.

Her mom puts her hands on her hips. "I'm fine, by the way. No stings to speak of, mercifully."

I fight the urge to tell this woman to pound sand or to wrap an arm around Eden. Emma clops past us into the house, and Eden tenses, her easy composure gone. "Hey," I say. "What can I do?"

Biting her lip, Eden closes her eyes and silently counts to ten, plump lips moving slowly. "Can you help me rearrange the freezer so all the honeycomb fits? I usually save it up to process in big batches on rainy days."

"Of course. I love rearranging freezers."

A laugh bubbles from her lips, her tense shoulders relaxing. My heart thumps an extra beat; thank God I can help. My track record of being helpful isn't much to brag about. We take our time until the ancient appliance is stuffed to the brim. Eden gets us some water and glances at the clock with a small gasp.

"Oh, shoot. I'm supposed to go duckpin bowling with Marsha. We're in a league..." She looks at me hesitantly, eyes wrinkled and cheeks turning red. "Would you want to come along? You won't be able to play... That's dumb, right? I shouldn't invite you if you can't particip—"

"I'd love to. Can I wear this?" I gesture at my mostly-clean t-shirt and dusty jeans.

"Sure. I'm wearing this." Her gaze tracks up and down my body and I might just clench my abs a little before she shakes herself out of it. "Well..." She looks down at the honey stains on her shoulders. "Maybe I'll change my shirt."

She runs inside, leaving me to wonder what possessed her to extend the invitation. One thing I know for sure is I'm not going to waste this opportunity to spend time with her.

10

EDEN

THE AIR CONDITIONING hits my skin like a cold, soothing squeeze when Nate and I walk through the doors of Pittsburgh Pinz to meet Marsha and the Honey Rollers. Nate laughed when I explained this was duckpin bowling—a miniature version of the game with short lanes, short pins, and a fast pace. At least, Marsha *insists* on a fast pace. "Keep it movin," she yells if the Honey Rollers get too chatty.

There are four of us on a team, all local beekeepers. I was lucky to be invited. Last season, Marsha called me in to sub for Devesh, who had to miss a game because he was driving to Tennessee to fetch a box of queens for the group. This year, Ghita asked to move to a rolling sub and, well, here I am.

Marsha waves from our lane along the back wall, and I tug Nate's hand, not thinking. He weaves his fingers through mine like it's a habit, and I halt in my steps to stare down at our hands. Nate sees me looking and pulls his hand away in a fist, like he's covering a cough.

We approach the table, and Marsha has pitchers of water and beer. Nate reaches for the water, and I make a mental note to ask him more about that, since he said he's changed his habits with alcohol since that unfortunate night we met.

I don't know what I was thinking that night. Eila and I were at a party in Polish Hill. Our mother had recently asked for money, we didn't have it, and she called us ungrateful brats.

I was emotional. Nate wasn't the only one hiding from parent issues with alcohol. Am I doing the same sort of thing now, inviting him here? This feels different from our drunken hookup. He stood up for me with the police. Mom isn't even promising things will be better this time, and I'm letting her walk all over me like a young kid desperate for her affection.

Is that how Nate sees me? Like a damsel in need of rescue?

Marsha pours me a beer and slides the cup my way. "It's that new IPA from East End," she says, her Minnesota accent coming through above the music and crashing bowling balls. Even though they're tiny and the lanes are short, it's just as loud as any regular bowling alley. But I get to wear my own shoes, and all the balls are the same weight. I don't have to remember which one is mine, because they're all about four pounds.

I take a sip of the drink, acknowledging Marsha with my eyebrows. "Oh my gosh. This is brewed with Eila's hops, huh?"

Marsha nods. "I guess I'm up on your sister's business more than you."

I laugh and take another sip. "It's really good. I'm so proud of her."

Nate arches a brow, and I explain my sister grows hops on vacant lots around the city—only two lots so far, but she has plans to expand—and she sells them to a local brewery. "Want to taste?"

I bite my lip as soon as the question is out, but he smiles and pours an inch or so of beer from the pitcher. He takes a small sip, sniffs, then takes another. His eyes don't give anything away, but he smacks his lips together and gives the mug an appreciative glance.

"Damn. That was well worth the one-year chip."

My stomach sinks slightly, my breath locking in my chest. Did I really just push him off the wagon?

But he gives me a playful nudge, letting me know he's giving me crap. "It's good. I never met anyone who grows hops before."

I nod. "You saw her plants when you were over helping me today."

Marsha whistles and claps for Devesh, who rolled a strike and turns toward me, face etched with concern. "This guy was at your house? Something happen with the wall project?"

Nate shakes his head. I can't bring myself to tell Marsha my mom kicked over the quarantine hive, that the queen flew off and took her girls with her.

Nate and I quickly exchange an entire conversation with eyebrow movements, and he says, "Eden forgot one of her buckets of spare beeswax and when I dropped it off, she showed me her setup."

Marsha downs the rest of her beer and holds up a

finger to Muriel, who is signaling for Marsha to take her turn. She leans forward, palms on the table. "When I get back, I'm gonna want to know your intentions with my protégé, mister."

She strides toward the lane and tosses a neat ball, pumping her fist while I flush and try not to make eye contact with Nate. Talk about mixed messages. I meant what I told him, though. I want to keep things professional, at least while he's my client.

He nudges me with his shoulder. I glance up at him, sipping his ice water, a smile in his eyes. "Just so you know," he whispers, mouth close to my ear, "my intention is to spend time with you, however you'll have me."

My stomach flips. I'm wearing dirty work shorts, and I'm sitting in a mini-bowling alley with a misfit group of urban beekeepers, and he wants to spend time with me?

He sets his water cup on the table and leans closer to me. "Maybe just the two of us." He holds up his hands. "Not that these guys aren't great. Nice roll, Marsh!"

My jaw hangs slack as Nate continues like he didn't just tell me he's interested in me. I know he asked me out, but then he saw me crying and watched my mother call the police on me. I keep waiting for him to take off running.

"She got her spare," he says. "Are you up next?"

I tuck my strays behind my ears and walk up to the lane, slapping Marsha a high five on the way. I wait for the green light to appear above the mini pins, and I throw the grapefruit-sized ball, knocking down six, which are attached to wires and get sucked into the ceiling. The dangling pins untangle and settle. As I wait for the green light to roll again, I glance over my shoulder and notice Nate laughing with Marsha. She pats him on the back.

He's so nice. I can admit that now that I'm not angry about having to take antibiotics. I was as much to blame for what happened. After all, I could have insisted we use a condom. I wasn't exactly sober when I pressed against him on the dance floor and whispered we should get out of there. We stumbled down the street to his house and had terrible sex, and I realize now I've been angrier with myself—and maybe my mom—than I ever was with him.

Nate gives me a thumbs up, and I smile, turning to face the lane. I'm certainly not angry now. No, I feel quite the opposite. I scoot to the left and roll, knocking down all the remaining pins for a spare. Marsha whistles alongside another whistle that's deeper, more resonant. Nate stands beside my mentor with his thumb and forefinger in his mouth, doing that sexy sort of whistle I never managed would be aimed at me.

But then my heart sinks when I see my mother sauntering toward our table with a weird expression on her face.

Nate stiffens. I slap an unenthusiastic low five to Devesh as he approaches to take his roll, and I make my way to the table. "Mom, what are you doing here?"

Marsha leans back, observing. Marsha's heard me vent about my mother a lot when we've been working together on beekeeping stuff. Marsha insists I need to find a skilled therapist, but I don't have health insurance, let alone anything leftover for a regular copay. If the drinks weren't cheap here at Pinz, I wouldn't even be able to join a bowling league.

Mom straightens her skirt and licks her lips, looking around with distaste. "I was in the neighborhood."

Obviously. I live around the corner, and she's bunking with me. I wonder which sister tipped her off about the bowling league. But then Mom notices Nate, and her demeanor changes. She rolls her shoulders. "I saw you at the house earlier. Big, strong hero come to rescue us from the bees, huh? Will you pour me a drink?" Mom flutters her lashes like a cartoon character, and bile rises in my chest.

Nate pours my mother a glass of water. She scoffs and shoves the cup to the side. "Eden, baby, I misplaced my house keys. I need you to lend me yours."

I breathe in and out through my nose. A locksmith is a great idea, but I'm not sure I'm allowed to do that as a renter. An urge to smack my mother bubbles inside my body, which I know is terrible, and I have to do something else with that anger. I close my eyes for a moment and think of calm memories, like pulling the bees from the picnic table at that wedding the other day. I felt proud and capable. Yes. That's the ticket. I'll channel that. "Mom, why don't I walk you home and let us both in. We can look for your keys in the morning."

She shakes her head. "No use." Her words are slurred, volume much too loud, even for a bowling alley. "I'm pretty sure they fell in the river today when I was on one of those tiki boats."

I clench my abs and turn toward Nate, who has his lips pressed tightly together. His fingers twitch on the table, and I wish he'd clasp my hand or something. "Um, when did you do a tiki boat ride? After you called the police about the bees?"

Mom rolls her eyes. "Don't be like that, Eden. They heard us screaming. They were in the neighborhood— because you don't live in a very good neighborhood. And if you must know, I was discussing a business opportunity with some investors. They took us on a ride."

Nate murmurs something under his breath, and I glance over my shoulder. It's my turn to bowl again. But I can't stay here with Mom like this, and I'm not going to give her my keys now that they're the only set to the house.

I reach for Mom's discarded water, chugging it down. Nate stands and leans over me, his mouth by my ear. "Can I talk to you for a minute?" He backs up without waiting for an answer. I gratefully step to the side with him and look up into his blue eyes. They almost glow in the dim light of the bowling alley. His lashes are so long and blond and curly. It's not fair for a man to have lashes like that. Eva would be jealous. She'd take his picture for her Insta posts.

"What can I do to help?" he says, and I return my focus to the situation at hand. I bite my lip and shake my head. I don't know.

Marsha taps her watch at me. I'm holding up the Honey Rollers. Nate takes my forearm gently in his hand, his thumb rubbing back and forth along my wrist. "Let me walk your mom home, and I'll bring your keys back here."

I want to puke at the thought of him alone with my mother. I can't imagine what she'd say, what she'd tell him about me. "Thank you, but that's not a good idea. She's—"

Mom is currently trying to whisper something into Devesh's ear, and he's offering her water. Marsha taps her watch. "Keep it movin!"

Nate licks his lips. "What if I stood in for you so you can take your mom home and let her in?"

"You'd do that?" I ask, gratitude washing through my veins in a cooling tingle. I never considered a solution involving Nate, despite him spending his entire day helping me with the beeswax.

He shrugs. "I'd rather walk you home safely, but given the circumstances... it seems like the way."

"Oh, thank you." Without thinking, I stretch up on tiptoes and hug him, pressing my face against his neck and sniffing briefly before extracting myself.

"Mom, come on." My voice is very different directed at her. I ran out of patience, plowing toward resentment. I grab my mother's shoulder and give one final glance back toward Nate after he finishes his first roll to back slaps from Marsha and Muriel. "See you tomorrow morning? We'll pull out the rest of the honeycomb."

Nate gives me a thumbs up and a grin, and I head home, my mother teetering behind me, rattling on about my lousy neighborhood.

11

———

NATE

EDEN'S BEE friends are so wholesome. At first it was weird when they kept asking me my intentions toward her, and then I really got to experience her mother up close and personal, and I appreciated Eden's got some real adults looking out for her.

I was honest with Marsha about my intentions: earn another chance with Eden Storm and make it count.

I'm wired when I get home from the bowling situation, so I head out to my garage. I'll burn off some energy organizing Dad's stuff.

My stuff...

The *business's* stuff.

One thing I'll say about hanging out with Eden is it's inspiring me to actually do things I've been putting off for way too long. She makes it seem possible. Before, it felt like too much to even open the garage door.

Dad would probably have smacked my ear if he saw all his tools in a jumble with wood bits. It doesn't take long to get each of the tools on its proper peg or shelf. It helps that Dad drew outlines of each tool or labeled the bins. Look at him... still making things easy for me from beyond the grave. No doubt he had a chart up in his brain for that, too.

The scrap wood resembles a Dr. Seuss cactus, each board sticking out of rubber tubs at odd angles, but I got it sorted by type, and that seemed more useful than sorting by size. It's creeping toward midnight when I see a beautiful chunk of pine I recently brought from the Morningside house. I smile, thinking of Eden working to pull honeycomb carefully from inside those walls.

She said something about having to quarantine bees any time she removes them from someone's walls or yard, and a quick online search shows me some of the tools beekeepers use. I think of the box Eden frowned at, all tipped over in her yard. I decide to make her a sturdier, temporary bee box. If her mom or a neighborhood critter gets at the box again, at least it won't leak honey all over the place.

I can't keep track of paperwork for shit, but the beveled edges on this project take me no time to cut and sand. I'm going to be dragging tomorrow, but this suit-case-sized box might make Eden happy, and that will keep me going.

SHE'S at the job site when I arrive in the morning, gorgeous in her usual tiny shorts and a tank top with the bowling alley's logo across her perky breasts. I'm grinning like a lovesick fool when I climb out of the truck with a thermos full of coffee. And then I stumble when I see her wringing her hands and breathing heavily in apparent distress.

"Thank you so much for everything yesterday," she says, rushing toward me. "My mom just... ugh. She was awful. Is *that* awful, that I think of my mom this way? I didn't give her keys because this is my only set—"

"Hey." I put a hand on her shoulder. "You don't have a single thing to apologize for. What your mom does is not on you. I mean, she cost you a colony of bees, right?" I give her a gentle squeeze, noticing her soft skin under my palm. "Would it make you feel better if I told you I have a present for you?"

"A present?" She blinks, shifting her weight and bouncing on her toes like I told her she won the lottery.

"Don't get too excited. I felt inspired after bowling." I open the passenger door of the truck, revealing the box. "I found a bit of scrap wood I thought might work for you."

Eden holds a palm over her mouth. She runs a finger along the wood, which I polished with some of the beeswax from her scrap bucket.

"You *made* this?" Eden slides the lid off and back on, admiring the grooves inside for the frames I always see her wrapping in rubber bands.

"Um...yeah." I scratch my neck, a little overwhelmed by the look on her face.

Eden yanks it from the truck and squats, resting the box on her lap. I burned *Storm Swarm* into the lid. I wanted to add a little bee or something, but I ran out of energy by that point.

"It's for your quarantine bees. I read that polishing it with wax would help waterproof it. I thought if something tipped it—" My words are cut off by a jump hug as Eden springs to her feet and leaps into my arms. She clings to me like a squirrel on a utility pole.

I can feel her along my entire body, heels on the backs of my thighs and strong arms looped around my neck. I return the hug gladly, wanting to wrap her up and never put her down.

"I love it so much, Nate. Nobody has ever..." Eden slides to the ground as if she just realized she jumped into my arms.

"You're welcome." My hands twitch on her waist.

Her cheeks turn pink, and she eases back, leaving my whole body cold and empty. "I'll put it in my van and meet you upstairs. We can pull out more honeycomb."

I nod and head inside, even though I want to wait and walk up the stairs with her. Maybe permanently fix myself to her side. I get my wish soon enough, though, as we are pressed together, lifting heavy sheets of waxy honeycomb from the wall and into Eden's cooler. We gently fill the entire thing, plus a few junk buckets, before Eden sits with her back against the wall, guzzling water.

I join her, chugging from my coffee thermos. Eden licks her lips, and I stare too long, not hearing at first when she asks, "How did bowling go after I left?"

"We didn't win, but only Muriel seemed upset. You didn't tell me we were playing for drink coupons."

"Everyone likes a good drink coupon." Eden fidgets with her bottle. "I'm just glad Mom didn't force a forfeit or something."

"I was happy to fill in. They were fun." We're silent a few beats. "How'd you meet the Honey Rollers?"

Eden chuckles. "I didn't really have a plan after high school. I was waiting tables, taking classes at the community college, but I wasn't feeling it. Esther had this rule where we had to be in some sort of school to keep living with her. I was terrified to tell her I left midway through the semester."

"Have I met Esther yet?"

Eden shakes her head. "She owns Bridges and Bitters in Lawrenceville. It takes up most of her time these days."

"I've heard of that place. Very fancy."

Eden sighs. "Yes, well, one day Marsha came into the café where I was working, all decked out in her bee gear and ordered an entire pitcher of iced tea. She'd been stung a bunch and was all sweaty. I asked her more about her situation, and she got me hooked up with beekeeping classes Muriel was teaching." Eden screws the cap back on the bottle, tossing it by her cooler. "That was four? Maybe five years ago. I quit the café about a year ago... right before I met you, I guess. But now my sister is moving out..."

I arch a brow, not catching her train of thought.

She frowns. "My sister paid half the rent."

"Ah, all the finances changed." I let out a low groan. "I feel you on that."

I help Eden haul the coolers and buckets to her van. She comes back up to do another check but declares the wall entirely bee-free. "I'll probably start processing everything this afternoon. I have a big order from the café where I used to work."

I peer into the wall and marvel at how many stinking bees were in there and how much physical product they created. There are still some bits and nubbins of wax along the wood, and I'm sure it's very sticky in there, but Chris will be excited to use a power washer before we redo the wiring.

I sigh and turn back to Eden. "I guess this is the end of our professional relationship."

She smiles, lips together. "Unless you find another swarm, yeah."

"Nice doing business with you, Eden Storm."

She holds out a hand, which I shake, but I don't let go. She laughs. "You, too, Nate Donovan."

I twist my wrist so I can rub her palm with my thumb. I can't let her just drive away without a plan to see her again. I already gave her the box. She doesn't seem to be flinching from my touch. "Do you want to go see a show with me this weekend?"

"A show?" She arches a brow.

"Yeah, like a music thing. Down at Hazelwood Green."

She presses a palm to her chest, emitting a little gasp. "I haven't been down there since they fixed it up."

"I'd love to take you. If you're interested."

"Like a date?"

I nod. "Is that okay? I'm not a client anymore..."

Her mouth tips up into a bigger smile, and I stand taller as a weight lifts from my shoulders. The air seizes in my lungs and I study her every movement, every flicker of her expression. She cants her hip, pink spreading through her cheeks. "I'd love that."

12

EDEN

MY MOM IS GONE when I get home from work. I stopped by with a new key for her in between errands, and she barely acknowledged me from the kitchen table where she sat, bent over her phone, still in her pajamas. Some of her stuff is in Eila's room, so I suspect she's out following whatever opportunity came up while she was throwing keys in the river from the tiki boat. And then she'll stroll back.

Before I can get too worked up about her leaving, Nate sends a text confirming our date for Sunday. I laugh at myself for keeping him in my phone as *Actual Satan.* I switch his contact info to his name and close the door to Eila's room. Better to worry about Mom later and focus on happy things for now.

THE REST of the week is a blur. I spend it at my house processing honey, cranking the vintage extractor, and bottling the amber product in the fresh shipment of jars with my custom label on the lids. Then I fill the food-grade buckets for my wholesale clients, and my freezer is officially empty.

Which means I need to check on the hives. I head to the yard Sunday afternoon, whispering greetings to the bees, thinking it might not be too bad living on my own. The extra honey from Nate's construction site project is like free money, and it should give me more than enough cushion for the rent once I get it sold.

"Hey, you." Nate's voice startles me from my mental math, and I jump, closing the lid to the purple hive. I almost have a full rainbow now since my quarantined bees from the wedding were healthy. I glance at the work clutter all around me; I'm sticky and smell like smoke. Nate grins, like he doesn't mind any of that. "I'm early."

I relax, although he can't be too early. I should have paid more attention to the time.

"Sorry," I start. "I can hop in the shower and be ready in a flash."

He holds up a hand. "I'm the one who's sorry. I tried to call, but I should have figured you had your head in a hive. Anyway, I came early to give you this."

He holds out a smooth wooden sign, etched with *Storm Swarm*, polished smooth with, I assume, beeswax. I touch the wood, fingers tripping over the delicate writing that matches the font on my labels. "Did you make this one, too?"

"I like making you things." He scratches the back of his neck, his eyes drifting to our shoes. "I like watching your face when you turn all pink like you don't know how to react."

I press a hand to my cheek, which is indeed heated. "Nate, this is beautiful."

He tips his chin toward the porch. "I thought I could hang it there, since you do all your honey stuff up in the mudroom. I can do that while you get ready."

My eyes fly wide. "Wow. That's... really thoughtful, Nate. I don't know what to say."

"How about you say you'll be down in twenty minutes, and then we'll listen to some sea shanties."

"Oh, is it that group of guys with beards? They're so fun."

Nate waves me on and gets to work hanging the sign as I shower and toss on a black jumpsuit I stole from Eliza. I braid my hair over one shoulder, figuring it will dry if it wants to, and pop in a pair of bee wing earrings Eva made after foraging the backyard and dipping her findings in resin.

I meet Nate out back just as he slides the power drill into a tool bag. He glances up and licks his lips. "You look beautiful."

I nudge him. "You also look beautiful." He's got on nice jeans, which means they're dark and a little tight in the butt. He's wearing a perfectly fitted t-shirt that says *I sneeze sawdust* with a union logo. He tops it all off with a pair of mirrored aviator sunglasses that really, *really* do it for me.

"Should we go?" Nate gestures toward his truck, and I climb in, watching happily as he puts the truck in gear and heads south toward the venue. We leave the windows open, enjoying summer air.

When we walk toward the event entrance, Nate puts an arm around my shoulder. I like it. I like being tucked against his side. Neither of us thought to bring a blanket or lawn chairs, but he has a flash of brilliance, and we grab a pair of buckets from the truck that we turn upside down and use as stools while we scope out the options.

Nate points to a family sitting near our buckets. "Is that lady mixing lemonade with iced coffee?"

I squint. "Yes. Huh. I never heard of that."

Nate scratches his scruff. "I don't think I'm ready to try it. But lemonade sounds good right now."

I bite my lip, wondering something, and decide to just go for it. "Can I ask you about the lemonade... Did you stop drinking entirely?"

"Not entirely. I realized I was abusing alcohol to cover up my grief. That's a line I got from the support group at the church."

I bite the corner of my cheek. "How often do you go?"

"Every week. At first, I felt like an asshole, just sitting there whining about having a dead dad." I wince but Nate pats my leg. "But I realized grief is selfish, and that's okay, and everyone there was hurting. It helped me to listen to other people talk about their own losses." He gives me a small, tight-lipped hint of a smile. "My dad would hate it... but I talk about my mom. She's still alive, but I have a lot of grief over her not choosing me, you know?"

I do know. I know it so deeply I shiver at the thought. "I keep waiting for my mom to leave again. I know it'll happen. She's gone right now, but I don't think it's permanent."

"Eden, you're not alone. I'm here to listen." He places a warm hand on my knee and leans his head against mine. "What will you do if she comes back?"

I'd love to think I'd slam the door in her face and change the locks, but I know I wouldn't. I feel stuck, destined to be the one bailing her out while my sisters learn to say no.

A ball of something big threatens to burst in my throat, so I point to the lemonade cart. "Let's get something to drink. And eat. I'm starving."

Nate nods and stands. We leave our buckets to claim our space near the stage and wander around the food vendors, choosing dumplings and pepperoni rolls. I notice a pizza truck has hot honey as a topping, and I make a mental note to see about infusing some honey with other things for the jars I sell on consignment.

Nate takes a sip of his drink and leans back, glancing down the row of food trucks. "You could make a killing here," he says, pointing to a table where a vendor offers soaps and candles. "Don't you make that kind of stuff?"

I shrug. "Yeah, but I think I mentioned there's a better return for less work if I can sell wholesale. I'm trying to think about a more dependable income, you know?"

He laughs. "I don't know. You see how I run my business. Right into the ground, basically."

"Oh, come on, you do nice work." I squeeze his shoulder. He guides us to our buckets, and we set out our array of food.

"Eden, I don't even know how to use QuickBooks.

Yesterday was the first I even *heard* of QuickBooks when Chris asked how it was going logging into my dad's accounts."

"Hmm." I do know how to use that accounting software, but I'm not about to rub that in his face after he trusted me with this knowledge. I can see he really feels like he's failing his team and his dad. "Well, like you just said to me, you're not alone, Nate." I nearly purr when his face softens. "If you want, we could work on paperwork together sometime. Give each other motivation to file the permits and check the budgets?"

"I'd like that," he says, stealing the last dumpling from the tray on my lap with flourish. The band starts, and I lean against his shoulder, swaying as the group sings old-timey songs.

They finish their set as we down the rest of our drinks, and the next group takes the stage. They play slow acoustic music. The sun sets along the Mon River, and the whole thing is sort of magical, taking place on a site that used to be a steel mill. It makes me think I could be revitalized, too, like maybe I haven't yet figured out my purpose, but that's okay. I can become something new and different. Maybe I can become someone who says no to my toxic mother, or at least insists she pay rent.

Maybe.

I lean against Nate, enjoying his warmth as the sky darkens and the soft hanging lights turn on. The band switches to a romantic song, and I look up at Nate. His breath speeds up and he stares at my mouth. I tip my lips apart ever so slightly, giving him the silent go-ahead to make a move.

And he does. It's so slow, so gentle I wonder if I imagine the whisper touch of his lips against mine, but he's just pulling back to check in with me. He waits until I smile before he goes in for real, wrapping his arms around me and pressing those sugar-sweet lips to mine. I ease my tongue into his mouth, loving the soft groan as his fingers spread across my spine. I shift my weight on the bucket, so I'm almost in his lap, one hand on the nape of his neck and the other on his sturdy shoulder.

I try to communicate my thoughts on fresh starts through the press of my lips and the sweep of my tongue. He groans again and then... he pulls back.

"What?" I gasp, blinking, dizzy. I can still taste him, sweet and salty at the same time, vulnerable and open.

He shakes his head. "I really like you, Eden."

"I like you, too. That's why I was kissing you..."

He tucks a hair behind my ear. "I'm..." He sighs and drags a palm down his cheek. I like feeling the stubble against the tender skin of my face while we kissed. I resist the urge to reach for him. "I don't want to be the guy I was before, using sex and drinking to cover things up."

I stiffen, not sure what to make of this confession. "Were you doing that tonight?" I want to understand. I was really enjoying our honesty, so I lean closer... try to convey I'm still on board for whatever this is.

"No." He turns my palm over in his lap, rubbing his thumb along my lifeline. "But I need you to know I'm trying really hard to do things differently... but I have no idea what I'm doing."

"Is that all?" I laugh. I can't help it. "Nate, I *never* know what I'm doing." I shift closer to him so we can talk above the music. It's intimate, especially here in the dark. I tell him what I was thinking about this venue, its transformation. "Can we work on our businesses together? I can help you use that software you hate."

The tension melts as he lifts his arm and settles it around me, pulling me tight against his side and resting his chin on the top of my head. "Definitely, Eden."

I can feel the whisper of his breath through my hair, the buzz of his voice vibrating against my back. We sit like that for the rest of the concert, soaking in the energy like noodles—transforming into something soft and tender.

13

EDEN

Esther wrinkles her nose at my goat-loving sister. "Eliza, please leave your boots on the porch." The boots do seem a little gross for indoors, especially at Esther's house, which is neat and tidy at all times. Eliza rolls her eyes but unlaces before collapsing onto Esther's couch as we wait for our brother-in-law to finish whatever smells amazing in the kitchen.

Family dinner at Esther's house is next level, and not just because she has matching chairs at her dining room table. Koa can really cook and thinks about things like how side dishes pair with various meaty main dishes. Sometimes Esther makes cocktails, but today Eila brought a bunch of beer since she just harvested hops and got a fresh batch from her brewing partner.

I soak it all in—the teasing and aromas and easy functioning—and appreciate how far we've all come in the past few years. Then I think about Nate last night, how we both have so much further to go but also how it felt to finally kiss him. How it felt to be open about our attraction to one another.

Eva throws a pillow at me. "Why does your face look like that?"

I throw the pillow back. "I have no idea what you're talking about."

She frowns. "Something's up. Tell us now, so we can focus on our food later."

Eva leans forward, elbows on her knees, like she's ready to guide an icebreaker activity. Eliza adjusts her posture on the couch so she's facing me a bit more, and Eila scoots toward me and drops an arm around my shoulder. "I've only been out of the house for like a week. Do you miss me this much?"

"First of all, Mom was sucking the air in the house." They all make matching groaning and understanding sounds. I tuck my hair behind my ears and sit up straighter. "I went on a date last night. With Nate."

"Diseased dick?" Eliza arches a dark brown and purses her lips. "When did we land on him as an acceptable person to date?"

"I'm begging you to stop calling him that." I tell them about the past week. Cleaning honey, subbing in for bowling, and his amazing handmade gifts. Hopefully I don't swoon too much.

Eva munches on crackers from a plate of appetizers that appeared. "What's the issue? You look... troubled."

I sigh. "It's a lot, you know? He's going through some hard stuff. We're both having similar issues with our businesses, with the paperwork and all that."

Esther pops her head around the corner from the

kitchen. "You're having business trouble, sissy? Why didn't you ask me for help?" She takes off her apron and folds it on her lap, joining us on the couch.

"I know you're there for me, Esther, but I also don't know where to start. I won't bore you with the details." I don't want her to take over. She always bails me out, and I need to understand how to do it myself if I'm going to keep this going.

Eliza snorts. "Oh, yeah, because I hate talking about urban agriculture." She pushes a finger into my leg. "You know I speak permit."

"That's true. But it's not the bee stuff. I don't know guys... I'm just overwhelmed. Eila moved out, and it got me thinking about who I am when I'm just me. Sure, I'm a crazy bee lady. But who else am I?" I hold my hands out, palms up. "Am I a doormat who lets Mom continue to treat me like crap? Am I a saint who rescues brides from swarms of stinging insects? Am I just a girl listening to music with a cranky carpenter who maybe didn't leave the best first impression?"

"You're *not* a doormat." Esther's tone is very assertive. "It's okay to be kind, but you don't have to tolerate it if Mom is being unkind. You don't owe her anything."

Eva nods and snuggles closer to Esther.

Just then, Koa taps his fingers on the doorframe from the kitchen. "Hate to break up the pep talk. Dinner is served, ladies."

Everyone gets up to walk to the dining room, and Eila stops to hug me on her way in. "You are still my best friend. You can call me or text me and all that jazz."

I smile, but we both know it's not the same wandering

into her room to lie on her bed while we unpack a situation. I have to start figuring things out on my own. Like what did it mean when Nate stopped kissing me? What does it mean to go slow on purpose?

My worries get drowned out in the chorus of praise for Koa's dinner—some sort of corn dish with seasoned beef. He paired a bread made from scratch that was so warm, the honey I spread changed viscosity within five seconds. Everything is garnished with lime and basil, like summer on a platter, especially with chilled glasses of beer.

I glance through the doorway to the kitchen, expecting it to resemble like a war zone since Koa made all this food. He catches me peeking. "I clean up as I go. Can't have the boss frowning at a mess, can I?"

Eila reaches for the salt. "Remember when Mom started that massive flour fight?"

Esther dabs at her face with a napkin. "Yes. And now I live in a house with a clean kitchen, thank you very much."

Eliza forks a mouthful of dinner and gestures with the cutlery. "It was fun, though. She decided we all needed to learn how to bake. Did we ever bake anything?"

Eva smiles behind her water glass. "Yeah, the place was a disaster, but Mom just laughed and said we were making 'snow angels' on the floor. We actually managed to make some pretty decent cookies."

Esther grunts, and we all turn to our meal, changing the subject to traffic and potholes and other Pittsburgh favorites.

I drive home happy and full, a container of leftovers for my lunch tomorrow sitting in the passenger seat. But as soon as I pull into the driveway, all the good feelings whoosh away. The front door hangs open, and my mom reclines in the living room, blowing smoke from her cigarette toward the open door.

"Mom, what are you doing?" I close the door and bite the inside of my lip, worried about how she'll respond to me leading off with a criticism like that.

"Well, aren't you all high and mighty." She stubs out the cigarette in the bottom of a plastic cup that probably had boxed wine in it. "Like this house is so fancy I can't smoke a single cigarette inside."

I cross my arms and try to appear bigger than I am. "It's my house, Mom, and I don't like the smell."

She waves a hand and groans, standing and flicking on the box fan. "Happy?" Mom points her index finger in my direction. "I expected more of a welcome when I got home from my seminar. Where have you been?"

I open my mouth to tell her I was at Esther's but decide against it. Her mention of a seminar confirms she's probably back in the pyramid scheme world, traveling to Vegas for expensive brainwashing with a side of Cirque du Soleil.

I take a deep breath to cool the boiling frustration on the back of my tongue. "What was your seminar like?"

"Well, now who's curious?" She clacks over to a box by the door, her wooden sandals popping against the hardwood floor. Mom opens a box full of tiny yellow cartons. "Voila!"

I'm afraid to ask, but the question rolls off my lips despite the fear. "Soaring Rejuvenation? What's that?"

Mom presses a hand to her chest, feigning overwhelm or disdain or something else meant to make me feel small. "I wouldn't expect you and your sisters to know about something high-end like this. It's cosmetics, darling. It's never too soon to worry about those frown lines, Eden. Are you moisturizing when you spend all that time in the sun?"

I press a hand to the skin by my lips. I didn't think people got frown lines in their mid-twenties, but I do also moisturize with some of the products I make from beeswax. "Can I see the box?"

Mom hands me a pot of night serum. "These are extremely high-end. We have many celebrities waiting to endorse this. Read those ingredients."

"Um, I don't really know what any of those are."

"Of course you don't," she says, snatching it from my grasp. "You're not a skincare scientist. But let me tell you, this is the good stuff." Mom dives into an obviously rehearsed speech, and I tune her out while I stare at the box. Realization dawns on me—she would have had to pay for the materials up front, as well as attendance at whatever sales pitch she went to.

"Mom, where did you get your startup capital?"

"I have my ways," she says coyly. "Why don't you give me some of the names of your friends so we can start setting up a party for them to learn about these awesome wellness solutions."

"I, um, don't have any friends." It's not a total lie, but I'm not giving my mother the contact information for my beekeeper mentors. My sisters are my best friends, but Mom should know that. Parents should know that about their children.

She arches a brow at me and pops her hip, resting a manicured hand on her shorts. "What about those people you were bowling with the other day?"

"Those are co-workers. Mom, you know I make cosmetics, right? That's part of my business? You're..." I drift off, not quite ready to call my mother a competitor as she stands here with a box of pyramid scheme products.

"Oh, you're worried I'm cutting into your bottom line." She taps her lip. "I'm sure we have a different target market, Eden. As I said, my products are very classy. Be a good helper and carry this to my room for me?" She clacks up the steps, leaving me next to her box of makeup.

I heave it into my arms and follow, stomach sinking as I enter her room and see two more crates stacked by the door.

14

NATE

THE MUSTY CHURCH basement smell smashes into me as I descend the creaky stairs. It's a scent I've grown used to—old hymnals, cheap coffee, and lingering incense. I pause at the bottom step, gripping the cold metal railing. Part of me wants to bolt, but I know I need to be here.

I push on the heavy wooden door to my grief support meeting and step into the dimly lit room. The circle of folding chairs is half-full of familiar faces. Some nod as I enter, others keep muttering to each other.

"Morning, Nate," DeJuan, our group leader, says. He's fiddling with Styrofoam cups and a large coffee urn. "Glad you made it."

I force a smile, settling into an empty chair. The metal is cool against my back, and I relish the opportunity to sit in air conditioning before work. These basement meetings always feel colder than they should, even in Pittsburgh's sticky summers.

As the stragglers file in, DeJuan takes his seat. He's a stocky guy in his fifties, with kind eyes and a permanent five o'clock shadow. "All right, folks," he says softly. "Let's get started. Who wants to share first?"

There's a moment of silence, and the regulars avert their gaze. I wonder if they're like me—worrying about hogging the floor, but also worrying about breaking down in tears. I stare at my hands, calloused and scarred from years of construction work. They're my father's hands. The thought threatens to overwhelm me, and I clench them into fists.

"I'll go," Kenya says from my left. As she starts talking about cleaning out her mom's closet, my mind drifts.

I don't want to be here. I don't want to be anywhere. The weight of the past year—Dad's death, the business, all the responsibilities I never asked for... It's *crushing* me.

Then there's Eden. God, the way I treated her initially. The way she tasted when I kissed her the other night. Can she really be serious about giving me another chance? I swallow hard, pushing the thought away.

Kenya finishes, and there's a murmur of support from the group. DeJuan thanks her and asks if anyone else wants to speak. The silence stretches on, broken only by the ancient HVAC system's hum.

"Nate?" DeJuan's voice startles me. "We haven't heard from you in a while. How are things going?"

My throat tightens, and for a moment, I consider lying. It'd be easier to say I'm fine, that things are getting better. But something in DeJuan's gentle gaze stops me.

"I..." I start, then falter. The words stick in my chest, trapped behind a wall of grief and guilt. I clear my throat and try again. "Things are... complicated."

DeJuan nods encouragingly. "Take your time. We're all here to listen."

I take a deep breath. "The business," I finally manage. "Dad's business. Donovan and Son. I'm... I'm not sure I can do it."

The admission hangs in the air, and I brace myself for judgment. Instead, I'm met with understanding nods.

"That's a lot of pressure," says Tom, an older guy who lost his wife last year. "Taking over a whole business, especially after such a loss."

A small weight release at having said the words out loud. "I'm making mistakes," I continue. "The paperwork, the management stuff... It's not what I'm good at. Dad made it look so easy, but I... I'm drowning in it."

"It sounds like you're carrying a heavy burden," DeJuan says softly. "Can you tell us more about what you're feeling?"

"Guilt." I run a hand through my hair. "Like I'm letting Dad down. He built this business from nothing, and now I'm messing it up. I can tell the guys on the crew are nervous. But at the same time, I hate dealing with contracts and payroll. I love building things, but I hate the rest of it, and I keep hoping it'll all go away... but it's piling up, and I know it's going to crash down on me."

There's a murmur of sympathy from the group. Kenya leans forward in her chair. "Have you considered that maybe this isn't what your dad wanted for you? To be miserable trying to fill his shoes?"

I blink, caught off guard by the question. "He named the business 'and Son.' It was his dream for me to take over." My mind flashes to a more recent dream, to Eden, bent over, studying the bees in that wall. I swallow hard, pushing the image away. "I've been so focused on trying to do everything right, to make up for ... for mistakes I made after he died."

DeJuan nods. "That's understandable. Grief can make us feel obligated to carry on exactly as our loved ones did. But that might not always be the best path for us, or what they would have wanted."

"But the business..." I protest weakly. "It was his life's work. I can't abandon it."

"Nobody's saying you should abandon it," DeJuan says gently. "But maybe there's a way to honor your father's legacy without sacrificing your own happiness and well-being. Have you considered other options? Maybe hiring someone to handle the management side while you focus on the construction?"

I shake my head.

"It's okay to forge your own path, Nate," Susan, a woman in her sixties, says. "Your father raised you to be your own man, not his clone. He'd want you to be happy."

Her words hit me hard, and a lump forms in my throat. "I miss him," I whisper, my voice cracking. "I miss being able to ask him for advice. He always knew what to do."

"Of course you do," DeJuan says softly. "And it's okay to miss him, to wish you could turn to him. But remember, Nate, your father gave you the tools you need. He taught you about construction, about hard work, and integrity. Those lessons don't disappear just because you might choose a different path for the business."

I wipe my eyes.

DeJuan gives me an encouraging smile. "Do you want to talk more about those mistakes you mentioned? About your progress making amends?"

I hesitate, thinking of Eden again. I want to trust that I'm making progress with her but I'm so raw after these meetings and grief still confuses me. "Not today." I'm overwhelmed by the possibility, by the suggestion of not continuing the management part of the business. I can barely make sense of my thoughts.

As the meeting wraps up, I linger, helping DeJuan stack chairs and clean coffee cups. "Thanks," I say quietly as we work. "For pushing me to open up today. I didn't realize how much I needed to say all that out loud."

DeJuan puts a hand on my shoulder. "That's what we're here for. Remember, healing isn't linear. There will be good days and bad days, but you're not alone in this journey."

As I climb the stairs out of the basement, the humid morning air hits my face. I take a deep breath. I don't have all the answers yet, but for the first time in a long time, I feel like I might be able to find them. And maybe I can find a way to make things right with Eden, too.

WORK on the house goes smoothly for the rest of the day, despite being distracted. Chris and Sparky are plowing through the flooring, and the electrical guy has come and gone, so we no longer need to run the generators. I'm good at this part. So why do I hate the rest of it so badly?

Someone has to do all the behind-the-scenes shit. My dad did it just fine.

Or did he? I think of how much he smoked, of how stressed he appeared most weekends when he thought I was distracted by the TV as he worked at his computer. Maybe Dad wasn't fine, either.

The thought works its way into my consciousness, and I have to shut off the jab saw. I can't cut drywall when I'm distracted. I peek at my phone, not sure who I'm hoping would have called. Nobody has.

But I think about Eden. I think about the feel of her in my lap Sunday night, the taste of her so perfectly sweet against my tongue. I need to see her.

I call her, but it goes to voicemail. I stare at the job site and realize almost everyone has left for the day. I drive home, shower, and cram a freezer burrito into my mouth before I try Eden again. When it still goes to voicemail, I pace the room, remembering her mother kicking over the bees. Eden's freezer is full now, and I hate thinking that something would happen to her hoard of honeycomb.

I drag a hand down my face, noticing the sprouts of stubble. What if Eden's mom kicked over more of her bees?

I decide to drive by the house just to say hello. She can send me away if she's busy.

WHEN I GET to Eden's house, all the lights are blazing but I don't hear any shouting. Thinking that's an improvement from the time I was here with the cops, I climb the porch steps and raise my fist to knock when the door pulls back, revealing a flustered Eden.

"Oh," she says, her mouth opening, and then her lip quivers. "It's you."

I lean against the doorframe. "I wanted to check in but your phone …" I hesitate, not wanting to sound like I'm accusing her of sending my calls to voicemail.

She closes her eyes. "My phone's dead. And I haven't had a chance to charge it because—"

"Eden, dear, are you coming up to help me organize these products? After all, I did help you with your bee work. Fair is fair, darling."

I raise my brows and peer over her shoulder. "Your mom's back?" She nods and I lean closer, needing to be near her. "Want to talk about it?"

She slumps into me, wrapping her arms around me in a hug that feels more like a cry for help. Startled I draw in a breath and gather her in my arms, squeezing gently and stroking her hair as she starts to cry.

"I got you," I whisper into the top of her head, smelling the faintest whiff of beekeeper smoke in her hair. "Do you want to go somewhere and talk?" She shakes her head against my shoulder, so instead of leaving, I scoop her into my arms and sit us on the porch. The boards creak under our combined weight, and I hold her until she seems able to talk. She tells me how her mom showed up with a bunch of pyramid scheme stuff that would have cost a couple grand out of pocket.

"I have the worst feeling, Nate. I don't know how she could have gotten the money in any above-ground way."

I reach for her hand and gently stroke my thumb

along her knuckles. "I hope this doesn't sound bad, but are you sure she didn't take it from you? Is there cash in the house?"

Eden sucks in a breath and sits up. "I used to keep cash in the freezer, with the frames. But I just processed everything last week, and I made a deposit."

The suggestion that her mother might steal from her has not insulted Eden, and I realize it's probably happened before. My guts clench in sympathy for this woman who is so good and so kind to even creatures that sting. "What do you want to do?" I run my fingers through her hair in a way I hope soothes her as much as it does me.

She shrugs. "I want to make out with you a little."

I laugh. "I guess when you put it that way..."

She reaches to kiss me, and I return the favor, nibbling her bottom lip and sweeping my tongue into her mouth. She moans softly, and I press a hand to the back of her head, holding her against me as we kiss among the fireflies outside.

Sooner than I'd like, Eden pulls away, breathless but smiling. "You're good at that," she whispers.

"Not half bad yourself." I let my thumb trace along her jaw. Her skin is smooth and soft, her lips swollen. Maybe from the stubble on my cheeks.

Eden nestles into my lap, resting her cheek on my chest. It's hot and the air is still, but I don't mind the extra heat of our bodies connecting. Quite the opposite.

"I just want my mom to be happy," Eden says, surprising me.

"Hasn't she always made you guys miserable?"

Eden nods. "Because she is unhappy. I know if she felt secure, she could be her best self and would make kinder choices with my sisters and me."

I think about her words for a long time, how Eden has spent a lifetime bearing the brunt of her mother's irresponsible choices. She still wants nothing but for her mother to live her best life. Eden is always doing that—making sure people are happy.

"Who does that for you?" I ask her.

"What?" She lifts her head, meeting my gaze.

"Who makes you feel secure and happy?" I cup her face with both hands. "Who takes care of Eden Storm?"

She bites her lip. "My sisters make me happy."

My eyes drift down her body before traveling back up. "But who makes you feel good, Eden?"

She blushes. My body springs into hyperdrive, my blood chugging south toward my crotch at the thought of her writhing in pleasure. Of Eden so lost to sensation she forgets her own name and can only moan mine. The hair stands up on the back of my neck and I have to touch more of her, I have to draw her closer to me. "Will you let me make you feel good?"

A flash of concern runs along her brow. "What about going slow?"

I did say that, but making her feel good feels necessary to me right now, not like I'm rushing into something dangerous. "I have no expectations, Eden. I'm here offering to make you feel good. Would you like that?"

She blinks, eyes owl-like. Her *yes* is a whisper—a barely perceptible nod of her head. I'm on my feet in a flash, carrying her into the darkness of the garden. The whole yard smells like honeysuckle, and the cicadas are screaming as if they're egging me on. I stride between her sister's plants and sink to the ground, hauling her tight against my lap as I suck on her neck.

I memorize the sounds she makes as my thumb finds her nipple under her shirt, and when my name is a shaking groan in my ear, I pull her against me, where I'm hard for her.

"I know what you need," I assure her. "I know you're not looking for complications or commitments."

My words seem to energize her, and Eden squirms against me, bucking and trying to find friction through my jeans and those tiny fucking shorts she always wears. I palm her ass as I reach up the leg of her cut-offs. Fingers greedy, I rub her pointed nipple with one hand as I squeeze her backside, grinding her against my erection, knowing it's not enough to pull her over the edge.

"More," she whines, and I growl in satisfaction. I bite her earlobe, earning a broken moan as Eden tries to muffle her cries against my neck.

She wriggles, kissing me and letting her head tip back when I slide my hand up her shorts. I trace the edges of her cotton underwear, and my fingertips inch inside.

"Oh, yes," Eden moans. "Nate, you feel so good."

"I'm going to take good care of you," I murmur. I find wetness, and she purrs in approval, kissing the column of her throat as she lets herself dip in my arms. "You're so wet, Eden. Your hot honey is seeping all over my fingers."

"Keep talking," she pants. "It's so hot when you talk like that."

I don't let myself wonder if I took care of her the first

time. I don't tax myself trying to remember then. Instead, I let the sight and sensation of her *now* burn into my brain, forming a core memory I will access when I touch myself for the rest of my life. Eden grips my shoulders as one of my blunt fingertips finds her entrance.

She lets me slide right in, and she whimpers in pleasure as I slowly fuck her with my finger.

"You like that? You ready for another finger, beautiful? That's it, gorgeous. Let me in. Shit, you're so slippery and perfect." The scent of her arousal fills the air, tart and salty, hanging around us like a mist.

"Look how you need this, Eden." I fuck her deep and slow with two fingers, and when she starts breathing heavy, I press against her clit with my thumb. She bows against my body, nipples pressing into my chest through both of our shirts, hard peaks desperate for friction. If we were inside, on a bed, I'd have her shirt off and use my mouth to bring her that much more stimulation on her chest. But we're in a garden, surrounded by fireflies, and both my hands are gloriously occupied.

She starts to pulse around me. She's so beautiful and sexy, letting herself trust me like this.

"It's so good, Nate." Eden's words are punctuated with breathy grunts. Her knees dig into my ribs, and I wince, but there's no way I'm slowing down when she's this close.

"It's a damn privilege to make you feel this way," I tell her. Eden's eyes lock onto mine and her mouth drops open in a beautiful pink *oh* as she comes apart. She trembles and shudders, shakes and pulses as she comes.

Nothing and no one has ever looked more amazing.

Eden collapses against my chest, sighing contentedly. I slide my hand from her body, bring my fingers to my mouth, and suck them clean, the taste of her blooming across my tongue.

"Fuck, you're incredible." I've never meant anything more truthfully. "Thank you so much."

Eden tips her face up, her eyes hooded and sleepy, arms draped across my shoulders and around my neck. "You're thanking me? For that? Shit, Nate. Give me a minute, and I'll take care of you."

"Nooo." I kiss her forehead. "I told you. This was for you. I wanted to make you feel good today. Now I want to tuck you into your bed, bring you a glass of water, and drive away knowing you'll have sweet dreams."

"Ha." Eden nuzzles against my chest. "Are you for real?"

"I could ask the same question."

"Mmm. So we're both real." She kisses my nose. "And you made me feel really, really good."

I hold her in the garden until I sense her start to doze off. It takes a bit of effort, but I get to my feet, adjusting her in my arms and making good on my promise.

15

EDEN

I'M FLOATING, I'm sure of it. I wake up so relaxed I barely react when my mother stumbles into the kitchen, grumbling that I didn't make coffee. Nate texts me to ask how I slept, and I flush from my ears to my toes.

ME

Like a dream. Thanks to you <3

NATE

I'm so glad.

I bite my lip and throw caution to the wind.

ME

I can't wait to repay the favor.

NATE

Favor? That was the hottest thing I ever saw. Trust me, I am satisfied.

Does that mean he doesn't want us to do things together? Or does it mean he was satisfied by himself afterward? I try not to worry about it and spend a blissful day pulling frames from hives all over the city—my own and the ones I take care of for clients.

What a shift, to intentionally not worry. Maybe I should seek pleasure more often.

I whisper to the bees, explaining that I'm having a terrific day and thanking them for all their work. By the time I get everything tucked into the freezer, it's almost bedtime, and I'm thinking of Nate and his magic fingers.

And his dirty mouth.

My God, the things he said last night...

I WAKE up to pouring rain that doesn't seem like it's going anywhere—a great signal to process all my honeycomb. I get myself situated in the mudroom with my new food-grade buckets, crank up the tunes, and prepare for that sweet wholesale honey income. Which reminds me... I really need to tackle paperwork, and a rainy day would be great for that.

I bite my lip. Would Nate want to spend the afternoon working on that stuff together?

I'm not even going to pretend I don't hope we could celebrate progress with another finger bang. Or more.

ME

Rainy day paperwork party?

I expect him to be working, not responsive, so I'm surprised when I see dots appear on the screen almost immediately as he writes a reply.

NATE

Seriously? That would be amazing. Meet
you around 3?

I send him a thumbs up without bothering to check if
my mother will be around this afternoon. That's probably
a mistake, but even if she says she's going out, I can't
necessarily count on that.

I contemplate this habit of hers while I crank the
centrifuge to spin the honey from the frames. It drips
through the filter into the bucket, mesmerizing me while
I realize my mother is always going to do what she wants,
when she wants. She's not going to become someone who
thinks about how her actions impact others… or
someone who can be relied on to be anything other than
unreliable.

It makes me sad. I stop spinning the crank and sit in
the chair, my legs splayed around the drum. I don't want
my mother as a roommate. The thought comes to me
with such clarity, like the translucent honey after it sheds
all its particles. I need to figure out how to ask her to
leave. I'm still sitting with that realization when I hear
footsteps on the porch.

I glance at the clock and see that it's nearly 3:00 pm,
and Nate is just a tiny bit early. I smile. Since we've recon-
nected, he's been one hundred percent reliable. Maybe a
hundred and ten, since he manages to be here when I
haven't even called him.

"Coming," I holler, heading toward the front door.

"Can you keep it down?" Mom hollers from her room.
"I'm practicing my pitch."

I don't bother to apologize. I greet Nate with a smile, which broadens when he leans in to press a soft kiss on my cheek.

"I missed you," he whispers.

I'm acting like a teenager who just got asked to a dance. This is the same guy I yelled at a few weeks ago, but it's also the same guy who made me come so hard I passed out on his lap.

"Let me clean up, and we can sit at the table in the kitchen," I tell him. He follows me through the house, setting a massive, ancient laptop on the table. He sees the extractor, where the last bits of honey drip from the spout into my final bucket of the day.

"That thing looks like it's seen better days." Nate runs a hand along the metal drum, staring in at the rickety clips holding the frames in place. I've converted half of the utility sink into a station to drain all the beeswax, so the honeycomb are clipped on string above a big basin with clothespins that have, indeed, seen better days.

"It's an antique." I give the ol' gal a good pat. "I bought it off Marsha when I was just getting started. She's been on me to upgrade."

I take a look at the bin beneath the wax, decide it's full enough to dump into the filter bucket, and get everything to a stopping point. I catch Nate staring at me as I lick a final drop of honey from my fingers, which of course takes me right back to the moonlit garden, remembering how he licked... *me* from his own fingers.

I clear my throat. "Let me show you some checklists I got."

I wash my hands, redo my ponytail, and settle in next

to him at the table. I get him connected to the Wi-Fi and show him some spreadsheets I'm committed to filling out. "My sister's friend Logan gave me some basic business maintenance to-do lists," I explain. "There are lists for each quarter, month, and week. Then she even made lists for how to do each thing if I get stuck."

His brows shoot up. "That's pretty generous of her."

"Big time. I think she's putting all the sheets together in some sort of course or something to sell as a side hustle. But for now, it looks like we should each... blech. File or check on permits and business insurance."

Nate's face brightens. "That's an easy win for me. I found the business insurance stuff on my dad's desktop, front and center."

We work quietly together for a while until I get distracted by the nearness of him. Heat radiates from his huge body, warming mine. When he moves his arms to type numbers or adjust the monitor, his forearm touches mine and sends sparks shooting all the way to my nipples.

Get it together, Eden.

I manage to register my beehives with the city and the state, and that feels like a huge weight off. Eila told me it took ages for the paperwork to go through on her vacant lot project, even with her City Inspector boyfriend moving things along. But this was an online process, and it was done in a few minutes. Man, I could have had this done ages ago. I marvel at how easy it was compared to what I'd built up in my head. I'll have to remind myself not to postpone things just because I'm scared it'll be time consuming.

I smile at Nate, feeling accomplished, but I pause when I see the frown on his face. The brightness has faded to stiff concentration and his lips press tightly together.

"Everything okay?" I place a hand on his arm and let my thumb trace an arc through the light hair there.

He groans and slams the lid shut on his laptop. "No, but I'm done thinking about it today."

He turns in his chair, and he's around me all of a sudden. His legs are outside mine. His hands rest on my thighs.

I like it. A lot.

I lick my lips and close my own laptop. "What do you want to think about instead?"

The grin on his face is pure sex, but I'm still surprised in the best way when he leans forward and says, "I can't stop thinking about how wet you were for me, Eden."

16

NATE

WORKING beside this woman is more complicated than I imagined. For one thing, she keeps smiling and humming as she trucks along, clearly achieving what she sets out to do. It's so sexy, seeing her confidence show up with this admin work the way it does when she handles the bees.

But also... my own work reveals how I despise what I'm doing. This is the first time I let myself fully form the thought.

I hate this.

I know it's the cost of owning a business, but it has all the appeal of a traffic jam to me, and I don't see a way through the zipper merge. Sure, I was able to renew the insurance. But everything on that spreadsheet of Eden's? Total mystery.

To avoid prolonging this exercise in humiliation—and because I really, really want to get my hands in Eden's pants again—I close my laptop and shoot my shot. Eden says she doesn't want to do anything with her mom around, and that's fine by me. I'm more than happy to drive her to my place, squeezing her thigh at red lights and enjoying the smiles and hot looks she sends my way.

We rush up my porch steps, and I have my keys out in record time.

"Oh, it's different," Eden says, peering through my open door.

"I forgot. You must have seen it... before." I scratch my head and hang my keys on the hook. "I cleaned up a lot— my act and the house." It took a few dumpsters, but I unloaded almost all my dad's stuff. He'd been hanging on to everything from his clothes from high school to crap my mom left before she split. I figure she was never returning for cracked old makeup if she wasn't showing up for her own kid.

Eden walks around the room, touching each of the photos I left on the mantle of me and Dad working together through the years. He was probably dragging me to job sites way too young, but he taught me everything I know. Dad made sure I was certified, which meant I actually could renew the insurance for the business.

"Do you want a drink?" I stand near Eden, sort of boxing her in against the wall. She seems to like it, leaning a little closer to me and licking her lips. She gives me a once over, and when she shakes her head no, I bend to kiss her.

It's on like a generator at a job site. Our bodies roar to life, pressed against each other. Both of us groan and grunt as we rip off each other's clothes. Thankfully I never open the curtains in my living room, because I am not stopping until Eden Storm is bare in front of me. When she is, I step back in awe.

"My god, you're beautiful," I whisper, trailing a finger from her collarbone, down her breast, to her navel.

She bites her lip. "You're nice to look at yourself."

The breeze from the ceiling fan picks up her hair and it flutters against my chest. Inspired, I wrap it around my fingers, giving it a gentle tug. With her head tipped, throat exposed, she looks vulnerable and extra sexy. I lick and suck at her until she moans my name.

"Nate, take me to bed," she whimpers. I grab her hand, tugging her behind me as I practically run up the stairs to my room. "Oh man, this is much cleaner," she says with a giggle as she dives into my bed. I don't even want to think about the condition this place was in when I had her here a year ago.

I pause, standing by her side. "I want to reassure you that I'm healthy," I tell her. "I've had checkups and, truthfully, I haven't been with anyone since that night... apart from you. In the garden."

Eden beams at me, eyes bright. "I'm healthy, too. Thank you for telling me."

I want to dive on top of her and smother her with pleasure, make her scream and come for days. I open my nightstand. "I have condoms," I say, setting a strip of them out.

"Excellent." Eden pats the mattress beside her. "I'm excited to get to touch *you* this time."

I lie next to her, giving her half my weight and propping myself on one arm. I rub and touch the expanse of creamy skin she's offering. Why can't everything be like this—hands on, tactile? I am so confident when I'm using my hands to create something, even if that thing is an exploding ball of pleasure inside Eden Storm.

She gasps when I skate a hand between her legs, but I do not linger. I chuckle and kiss her. "Be patient, and you'll get what you're looking for." I press my lips to her shoulder and then peck my way down her body until I'm nestled between her legs, which she bends and tips open. She sighs as I arrive at her center, where I pause to drink my fill with all my senses.

I've been imagining what Eden looks like. Each night when I touch myself to the memory of her coming on my hand, I think about how those curls I felt would appear, how her folds would be wet and puffy from my attention.

"What are you doing?" Eden props herself on an elbow and glances down at me, brow furrowed and lips pursed to one side.

"Memorizing the look of you." Before she can comment, I spread her open with a few fingers and lick. Her taste is familiar, seared into my brain from the other night. There's just more of it now—as much as I want with her spread open for me. Eden wriggles on the bed as I lick her. To my surprise, as soon as I slip a single digit into her slick center, she comes instantly.

"*Nate!*" Her eyes flutter shut, her mouth set in a gorgeous O that will be seared into my mind forever.

I rub her thighs and kiss my way up to her shoulders as she calms down until she sits up abruptly, fussing with her hair. "Give me a second, and I'll reciprocate." Eden tries to tie her dark waves, and I place a gentle hand on her wrist.

"You don't have to rush, and I don't need you to suck me off, Eden."

She flicks one of my nipples. "Is that what you thought I meant?"

I shake my head and swat her behind. "Cheeky."

Eden tilts her head to the side and reaches for me. I hiss when she wraps her hand around my length and traces her thumb through the pre-cum gathered at my tip. "I'm ready to be serious now."

She kisses me, a groan slipping from her throat. Her tongue slides deep in my mouth, tasting her sweetness. She matches the strokes of her wrist with thrusts of her tongue until I'm about to fall apart.

"Hey," I say, pressing my forehead against hers. "I'm close, Eden."

"I see." She withdraws her hand and then fusses with the condom wrappers. "We'd better move on then. I want that thing inside me as soon as possible."

She rips open the wrapper and slides the condom onto my dick. I roll to my back to give her easier access, eyeing the amused grin teasing her kiss-swollen lips.

"What's funny?"

She shakes her head. "Nothing. I just never thought I'd be here again and..." Her grin widens. "Now I can't imagine being anywhere else."

All the change of the past year flashes through my head, all the work and assumption that I was always just going to be swimming in that same fog. But she's right. This is right—this is perfect. "Come here." I tug her so she's straddling me, hands on my shoulders, mouth against mine. I kiss her until my hips move toward her slick center involuntarily, and before I know it, Eden slides down onto me, impaling herself with deep moans and squeezing my ribs with her knees.

Our bodies come together perfectly, tight and wet. I rest my hands on her hips, letting her set the pace and move in ways that feel good for her, because everything about this feels incredible to me.

"This is so perfect," I grunt. "Can't believe how good we are."

"So good," she says, head thrown back, eyes closed. There's no way I'm looking away from the sight of Eden Storm riding me, perky tits jiggling as she moves, hair everywhere, face lax with pleasure.

I reach up to rub her nipples, and she gasps. Her eyes fly open and meet mine. When I squeeze a little harder, she starts shrieking my name, grinding hard against me, milking my cock with her inner muscles. Then she comes in a beautiful, brilliant spasm that has me falling right over the edge with her.

My heart pounds so hard I'm sure she can hear it. Eden tips forward against my chest and places a hand above it. Her own breathing is fast and rough, and we lie together, still joined, until thoughts feel possible again. I press a kiss to her cheek and deal with the condom, stopping in the bathroom to grab a washcloth and run it under warm water.

When I start to dab at her body, Eden purrs like a cat, stretching in the bed. "This is so nice."

"I like taking care of you." I consider throwing the washcloth on the floor and playing with her clit again, but Eden's stomach growls.

"And you're hungry," I say. "Let's make sandwiches."

17

EDEN

Sleeping with Nate—and then sleeping over with Nate—felt so natural. I already can't imagine life without his scratchy cheek against my shoulder while I'm falling asleep. Being taken care of is so intoxicating it takes me a few days to realize I'm letting myself be pampered.

The man makes me food. I see now why Esther keeps Koa around.

I skip everything but work, even family dinner, and spend the week with Nate, curled up on his couch with our laptops or watching fireflies from the overgrown pedestrian stairs in Bloomfield. I think about how easy this feels, how pleasant, and I remember what it looked like when Esther finally opened up to Koa. She said something like she thought she was protecting herself by not letting anyone in, but she never realized she was missing out on an explosive reaction when two people really connect.

I see it now, enjoying the ravine behind the Bloomfield pool, at the landscape strangled by knotweed. Nate weaves his fingers into my hair, and I don't feel smothered. I feel rooted.

It's kind of a pain driving to Nate's house every evening after work, but there's no way I'm going to invite him to sleep over while my mother is staying with me.

It's a problem. I just don't know how to do anything about it. She's not even paying me rent, and I'm the furthest thing from comfortable in my own home. Plus, I keep waking up extra early at Nate's because I need to rush home and make sure Mom isn't doing anything to the bees. Not that she is awake when I get there.

Apart from that, I spend a perfect week working on my beeswax cosmetics during the day, eating dinner with Nate, having orgasms with Nate, and then sleeping in his cozy bed, enjoying his air conditioning and snuggly presence all night. He hasn't really agreed to co-work on admin stuff for our businesses again, but I've been chipping away at my to-do list while he watches the Black Sox lose. Apparently, Pittsburgh hasn't had a good baseball team in decades.

But when Monday rolls around, I'm faced with the decision if I'm going to bring him to family dinner with my sisters. I'm already laden with guilt over sneaking out, so Mom doesn't ask where I'm headed and crash the party. Esther has been very clear Mom's not welcome at our sacred sister meals.

What does it mean if I bring Nate? What does it mean

if I don't? I smack the snooze button on my phone and lie in his arms, worrying.

"What's up?" he asks, his chest rumbling beneath my ear. "You seem restless."

I roll to face him. "How can you tell?"

He chuckles. "You're literally wriggling around, and I'm not catching vibes from you that you're looking to get frisky this morning."

"Is it really morning?" I peek at the crack between the curtains, worried I set my alarm for PM or something. The sky is just barely turning gray. I realize we are heading fast toward autumn and less daylight. Late fall and winter are much slower times for me. I could deliberately save up my admin stuff for the winter months when I don't have as much hands-on work with the hives and the honey.

"It's morning enough." Nate stretches. "What's bugging you? Want to tell me while I make the coffee?" He stands next to the bed, naked, scratching himself. It shouldn't be sexy but sort of is. He's so comfortable with me. It's vulnerable, and I really like it.

As he bends to pull on a pair of shorts, I blurt, "Will you have dinner with me and my family tonight? Not my mom. My sisters. At Eliza's house. There will be goats."

His mouth crooks in a grin. "Of course. What should I bring?"

I wave a hand. "Oh, you can't bring anything there. The goats will eat whatever it is. They're absolute monsters. Although... they're supposed to be out on job sites. Hmm."

Nate walks down the stairs, shouting over his shoulder. "You're going to need to tell me more about this goat business."

I follow him, tugging one of his t-shirts over my head as I pad barefoot to his kitchen. He turns, coffeepot in hand, and his mouth drops open. "Is that my shirt?"

I nod. He sets the pot on the counter and strides over to me, surprising me with a fierce kiss. "You look really freaking hot in my shirt." He slides a hand around my back and lifts the hem. "Just the shirt? Christ, Eden."

I rest my palms on his chest. As always, he's warm, and I rub my fingers in the fuzzy blond hairs above his heart. "You're easy to impress."

He shakes his head. "Everything about you is so impressive."

The coffeemaker beeps. "Shit. I didn't add the water." As he rushes to get caught up, I text him my sister's address. By the time I leave to get to work, I've promised to wear his shirt to dinner and compromised that I'd be wearing shorts and a bra with the ensemble, at least until he gets me back to his house.

I ARRIVE at Eliza's early since I was dropping a case of beeswax salve at a shop near her house. Her property gives a little supernatural vibe; one minute, I'm driving through neighborhoods and past hospitals and bars, and the next, I'm creeping along an unpaved road, and electric fence and companion donkey greeting me. Eliza's in the city, but she had vacant lots on either side of the shitty house she bought. Once she owned the whole parcel, she had enough land to legally keep goats.

"Hey, Chiron," I say as I park. Eliza's evil donkey approaches the fence, which isn't buzzing, so I risk leaning in to pet the little gray menace.

My sister's head appears from the shed by her house. "Oh good. You're early. Would you rather muck out the shed or get the pasta started for me?"

I roll my eyes. "I'm not shoveling poop for you. Also I'm bringing someone to dinner, so I'm putting in an extra box of noodles."

"Someone, eh?" She waggles her brows. "Does this someone have a history of making bad choices?"

"Can you not? We have something really good going on."

She flaps a hand at me, and I make my way inside. Eliza's house, like mine, has seen better days. Many of the older houses in Pittsburgh are brick, but she's got one with wood siding that appears to have been gnawed on by livestock. Inside, she's refinished the hardwood floors and fixed the original kitchen, so it's like some sort of farmhouse people would see in a movie about pioneer times.

I get the gas stove lit with a pack of matches from Esther's bar and hum to myself while I chop veggies. Eliza left detailed notes on the counter for her meal plans, so it's not too hard to get the grilled chicken cubed pretty quickly while I boil the noodles. She set out a dressing for the pasta salad and I love that my sister topped the jar with one of my beeswax-cloth malleable coverings. I set a hand over the top to give the dressing a shake, then carry the whole cauldron of pasta salad to the table and glance out the dining-room window.

I freeze, seeing Nate out there in his toolbelt, talking over his shoulder to Eliza as he... fixes her shed.

I step out the back door and shout over the braying Chiron. "What are you two doing?"

Eliza smiles, walking closer so she doesn't have to yell at me over the noise of Nate's power drill. "Your boyfriend is fixing the gate to the pen. The girls have been getting out more than they ought to. There was actually a meme going around from when Persephone was munching dandelions at Fowler playground."

I cross my arms over my chest. "Can you *please* not call him my boyfriend?"

Eliza reaches for me and tugs at Nate's shirt, that I'm still wearing. She flaps the material around like she's waving a flag. "So this is *your* giant shirt? Not something you'd borrow from a boyfriend?"

I swat her hands away and tie the shirt in a knot. "Shut it. Don't call him that or the other thing. Can we just call him Nate and let him be a guest? I can't believe you put him to work."

She throws her hands up. "Woah now. He offered. He pulled up in that sexy truck, gave a wave, and then Chiron smashed through the fence to lick his face. It was super cute. I took a video."

I want to see that video, but I also want to make sure Nate isn't freaked out. I walk outside, gingerly avoiding small piles of goat poop in the yard. Esther shows up with Koa and Eva in tow, and soon, Eila and Ben arrive.

There's a whole row of Storms just watching my unaware boyf— *Nate* bent over, tightening screws.

My feet carry me toward him unbidden. "That should do it," he says, giving his drill a cute twirl before tucking it in the loop on his toolbelt. He turns, muttering something about the triangle placement on the gate being sturdier, but he notices his audience and halts in place. "Oh." He waves. "Hi."

18

NATE

Eden has a strange look on her face when she follows Eliza and me inside the house for dinner. She's quiet as her other sisters compliment Eliza on the meal, which gets my goat; I'm pretty sure I saw Eden in the house cooking.

I'm the last person to butt in on family drama—or potential family drama—so I take a risk and drape an arm around Eden's shoulder as I fork a huge bite of pasta salad. "This is great," I say, and her smile is both electric and a little confused. "Everything okay?"

She takes a deep swig of water. "You fixed my sister's shed."

Esther perks up at this opportunity to tease Eliza and she turns to face me. "I still can't believe you put yourself near Chiron on purpose."

Eliza slams her mug on the table. "He's a donkey who acts like donkeys are supposed to act. Don't be upset that he bit through *one* pair of jeans, Esther. You shouldn't have startled him."

"Oh, excuse me. I forgot that walking up the path to the porch with a pan of lasagna is bothersome for a farm animal in the city."

The women bicker a bit, and I soak it all in. This is already a great experience for me. I grew up with just my dad. There were occasional meals with some cousins at my grandma's house, but we don't keep in touch. The Donovans don't have anything like this weekly communion the Storm sisters have going on.

When there's a lull in conversation—mostly due to people giving each other the finger with both hands and Koa demonstrating how Māori people stick their tongues out for a similar emotional intent—I clear my throat. "Thank you all for having me for dinner. This is pretty cool you do this every week."

Ben raises his eyebrows and gestures at the bickering. "Is it cool?"

"Absolutely." I raise my glass. "Cheers."

Esther brought a big vat of a new non-alcoholic cocktail she's testing for her bar. I don't know whether Eden said anything about me not drinking much or if Esther actually does rotate through some NA options, but I love we all have the same drink with the same meal. It feels cozy, damn it.

Unlike everything else in my life.

I got here early because I couldn't take it at work anymore. No matter how many evenings Eden spends on her computer next to me, offering to help, I'm overwhelmed by it all. I'm messing up payroll with my crew, and I haven't been doing a good job keeping the Morningside property owner informed. He's threatening to fly to Pittsburgh to see the place in person.

Eden elbows me in the side, and I realize I've zoned out. "Sorry. What?"

"Esther asked how you fixed the gate."

I furrow my brow. "I don't want to sound like a jerk, but mending a gate is a pretty easy lift for a contractor. You should see me pulling honeycomb from in between attic joists." I grin and squeeze Eden's thigh, then leave my hand there, enjoying the fact that she lets me. This sweet woman wore my shirt, as promised, and it looks so good tied in a knot at her hip. I want to bite it loose.

"Oh," Eva says, resting her chin on her hands. "How is all that going? With the bees in the house and rescuing the honey they left?"

Eden swallows her cocktail. "I processed it all the other day. Stuck it in buckets and dropped it with my wholesale clients. I'm going to do cosmetic stuff now that we're closer to fall and it's not quite as stifling all the time. I just hope Mom doesn't go snooping around my stuff while I'm out of the house." She bites her lip; she's more than a little concerned about this possibility. I'm not sure if her sisters even know Emma kicked over one of Eden's hives and made her lose that whole colony.

Esther points a fork at Eden. "You need to get Mom out of that house. You shouldn't have to worry about your livelihood."

Eliza smacks the table in agreement. "Has she said anything about when she's moving on?"

"Oh, like she ever says anything." Eila shakes her head and crosses her arms over her chest. "I'm not sorry I moved out, because I love living with you, Benny." She pauses to squeeze his arm, startling him, before turning her attention to Eden. "But I am sorry you took Emma in and brought all that energy into your house."

Eden takes a shaky breath. "It really is kind of bad," she whispers. "She's always critiquing the house, criticizing the food I don't make. And I know I don't have to say this, but she's not contributing anything to food or rent."

"Then send her a bill," Esther says. "Or tell her to get the hell out. Look, Eden, I know you have a whole thing about keeping peace and thriving off harmony, but enough is enough. What kind of adult mooches off her kids after failing to take care of them properly?"

Eliza sighs through her nose. "Want me to go throw all her shit to the curb? Her cases of shitty makeup she's trying to sell?"

Eva's eyes go wide. "She's selling makeup now? Ugh, from the same house where Eden's making cosmetics?"

Four of the Storm sisters keep going, airing decades of grievances against their mother, while Eden simultaneously stiffens and shrinks into her seat. "Want to get out of here?" I whisper into her ear as Koa tries to get everyone to stop arguing about their fantasy methods to destroy their mother.

Eden swallows. She says to the table at large, "I should get going. Not just because I need to check on my stuff, but I want to get an early start tomorrow. I'm working with the propolis oil to make some tinctures for that boutique on Butler Street."

"Oooh, I heard about that," says Eliza. "One of my farmer friends is using it on cow udders to treat mastitis."

Esther throws her napkin on the table. "Okay. Cow mastitis is my cue to exit." She tugs Koa by the hand and throws a wave over her shoulder.

Eila, Eva, and Eliza are undeterred. Eila licks her teeth and frowns. "I kind of want to see this stuff, but I have to be at the cemetery all day tomorrow. Will you still be working on it after four?"

Eden shrugs. "I doubt it. But you can check it out. I'll give you a little nibble, if you want."

"I want to do some reels for you," Eva says. "This is the kind of weird shit that goes viral. Bee oil? That treats cow udders?" She rubs her thumb and forefingers together like she's gesturing for a wad of money.

Eden points an index finger at her sister. "Guys, I'm not marketing it for animal husbandry. I'm marketing it to affluent granola people who shop on Butler Street."

"We're coming. I can bring dinner. Might as well make it a demo night. Maybe Eden can stick bee venom in our lips and plump us all up." Eva bats her lashes at Eden, who rolls her eyes.

"You guys are weird. And I love you. Of course you should all stay for dinner and try out my CBD beeswax salves." Eden meets my gaze, extending a silent invitation. My fingers itch to stroke her chin.

"I wouldn't miss it. But I have no idea what you're talking about."

Eva grabs at the hand I raised to cup Eden's cheek. "Look how rough his paws are, Eden. We can make a video of you rubbing palm balm into his skin, really talk up the magic properties of your Storm Swarm. The business name even sounds manly."

Eva rattles off a bit more marketing advice before we all manage to clear the table and make our way to Eliza's door. Chiron brays from the now inescapable shed.

I walk Eden to her van and lean an arm on the roof, hoping for a goodnight kiss. She seems uncertain and stiff. "How can I help?"

She gives me a small smile. "I just... need to grow a backbone. About my mom."

"She has overstayed her welcome."

Eden winces a little, and I wish I hadn't spoken up. I guess her sisters piling on didn't help her confidence in setting a boundary there.

"Want me to come over while you talk to her?" I offer. "I could wait outside, or..."

She shakes her head. "Just coming tomorrow for the propolis party is enough. It'll give me something to look forward to as I psych myself up to ask Mom for rent."

"Rent is a great start." I press a kiss to her cheek. "You got this."

She clutches my hand. "You'll really be there? To see the propolis?"

"Of course." Eden waves as she drives away.

I LEAN against my truck as I watch Eden's van, surprised by how excited I am at the idea of a cosmetics party with this woman and her sisters. I pull out my phone to write it on my calendar so I don't forget, when I see a text from Kenneth The Jagoff.

On a flight tomorrow at 2. Be at the
property by 3. I expect results.

I mutter a curse, then apologize to the only one in the vicinity—the donkey. I'm going to have to face some very serious realities in the morning.

19

EDEN

I DON'T HAVE the energy to say anything meaningful to my mom when I get home. She's taken over the dining room table with her boxes of things, organizing into piles and talking to herself when I step through the front door. She holds up a finger to shush me, which draws an involuntary groan from my throat as I walk past her for a drink of water in the kitchen.

I'm supposed to have a talk with her. I'm supposed to ask her for rent. Her silencing finger quiets all the bravery I built up. Dejected, I head to bed.

I WAKE up with the sun shining and birds chirping and a revitalized sense of power.

I can do this. I can give Mom an ultimatum when she wakes up, then I'll spend the day making cute jars of beautiful bee products. I start thinking about Nate's rough hands. It would be interesting to make a special product for people who work with their hands... maybe from the wax I saved from the construction site.

My mind is buzzing, much like all my gorgeous friends outside. I skip into the mudroom to pull the wax from the freezer.

My feet trip over a cord, and I furrow my brow, my stomach dropping into my feet. Someone unplugged my freezer. I open the lid. Everything inside is a melted, re-solidified lump. It has to have been at least a day—probably longer.

I clutch at my chest. This is fine. There's no honey in here. I can figure out how to melt and purify the wax. I just need to make sure I don't damage the equipment and frame pieces in the process.

A tear stings at my eyes, and a humorless laugh tumbles from my lips. I never get stung, but this situation hurts like I've been stung a million times all at once.

"Oh, there you are. We need to talk."

I whip around at the sound of Mom's voice.

She stops short at the tear on my face. "What's wrong?"

"What's wrong?" My once controlled anger has been uncaged. Too bad Nate didn't reinforce this one. "The one rule I gave you when I opened my home to you was to not touch any of my things. And you unplugged my freezer."

She pushes up on her toes, peering over my shoulder. "Oh, that? I had to. It was making noise."

"Making noise?" I'm sure my face betrays the depth of my anger at this situation. My throat tightens and my ears raise. All the tendons in my neck flex, and I'm not sure I ever let myself get visibly angry around my mother before.

"Oh come *on*." She groans like a teenager. "I was working on my pitch on a video call, and it was rattling. I must have forgotten to plug it back in. It's not like you had food in there." She walks away like that's the end of the discussion, but I lunge after her and grab her arm.

"Mom. It's my work freezer. What do you think I do for a living?"

She frowns at my hand on her arm and shakes herself loose. "I have no idea, Eden. Something to do with sending a horde of bees after your mother. You told me you sell honey. There's no honey in that freezer."

"This is unacceptable behavior," I blurt. "This just isn't how adults behave. I'm sorry."

As soon as I add the apology, I wish I hadn't. She'll see through my bravado. She'll finagle her way into my sympathy. I clench my abs and frown at her.

"And where do you expect me to go on short notice? I'm on the cusp of a rush of sales. You haven't even shown the slightest bit of interest in my business. And I was going to let you invest at a bargain, too." She sniffs aggressively.

"Invest? With what money, Mom? I told you I'm struggling to pay rent since Eila moved out. And you're here, running a competing cosmetics racket, while I'm trying to sell boutique beeswax products to local businesses. And you're *not paying rent*. This is just..." I wave my hands around. "This is not okay."

I want to scream. All the years of her doing whatever she wanted and leaving whenever there were messy consequences… I hear a creak, and the front door opens. I turn to see Eva and Eliza, standing there clutching hands, faces stiff with concern.

"We heard yelling," Eva says. Neither of them looks to Mom—they're here for me.

Clarity settles in my chest, like someone wiped away a smear of honey from my brain. We all agreed not to let our mother interfere with our businesses, and they came here to help me with mine. I know what I need to do.

I let go and roar at Mom, "You need to *get out*."

There's silence as the final *t* in the word rings in the air.

Mom spins to face my sisters. "Your sister here is throwing me out. Can you believe it? Over a janky hunk-of-junk freezer."

Eliza smiles at me. "You kicked her out." I can feel the thumbs up she's sending me mentally, and a small flicker of hope spreads behind my sternum.

Mom either ignores or is completely oblivious to Eliza's smile. "Yes!" she says to my sister. "Can you fit my things in your truck, dear? I need to stay with you. Ugh, this will throw off the meetings I have this week, so it'll be who knows when until I get this show off the ground and—"

Eliza holds up a palm a millimeter from Mom's face. "You are not living with me. You are not allowed to even know where I live."

Mom snorts. She starts yelling at Eliza, and it all blends together in a rush of overwhelm until I realize Eva has walked me to the kitchen and plunked me on a stool. "Here," she says, shoving a glass of water toward me.

I chug it down and whimper a little. "Mom has never cared for anyone but herself," I mutter. For years I kept thinking if someone just showed her kindness, she'd respond with more of the same. But I think it's too late, and Mom is too damaged. "You're all going to say *I told you so* about me letting her stay here, aren't you?"

Eva shakes her head. "Unless by 'all' you mean Esther, who might say it. But I doubt it." We jump when we hear the front door slam. Someone drags something heavy down the wooden steps outside.

Eliza pokes her head in the kitchen. "She's gone, Eden. Good job kicking her out."

"Did I do that? Did I throw our mother out to live on the street?" I shake and cry, and Eliza and Eva wrap their arms around me, trying to comfort me. I can't tell if I'm experiencing relief or regret.

Eventually, Eliza opens the cupboard under the sink. She pulls out a pair of yellow dish gloves and snaps them on.

"Right," she says. "Tell us what to do to clean up the beeswax."

"I'm not going to lie," I tell my grief group as everyone slurps coffee. "I have no idea what to do here."

DeJuan nods and waits for me to continue. I told them how I've been thinking about hiring a business manager. I've been floundering with paperwork, the property owner is showing up today, and I promised I'd help Eden make hand cream or whatever it's called.

"I'm pulled in too many directions. I'm not cut out for this."

Kenya leans forward. "You know you don't have to do anything you don't want to, right? It's okay to quit things that make you miserable."

DeJuan holds up a hand. "The word quit can carry negative connotations. But Nate, Kenya is right—you don't have to continue doing something you hate. You do not owe your father a lifetime of work in a field you don't enjoy."

I drag my hands through my hair. If I don't run Donovan and Sons Construction, what the hell do I do?

The meeting continues with others sharing about their lives. It's been interesting for me to learn about how things in my life that feel unrelated—like work—can all be affected by grief. I wonder if I feel a block to this work because I miss my dad.

When the meeting wraps up, I head to the job site, not any closer to a path forward. Sparky waves from the porch as I climb next to him. I give him plenty of space because he's trimming quarter rounds. The guys must have made a lot of progress if they're already prepping the trim.

"Nice, Sparky." I toss him a salute on my way inside.

It looks good in here. Not as bad as I thought earlier when I lay awake, tossing and turning. I spy Chris over in the kitchen with the granite guy and make my way toward them. I insert myself into the conversation, and before I know it, hours have passed as we get the final estimates for kitchen fixtures.

Chris and I are bent over the plywood placeholder counter, staring at numbers, when Kenneth the Jagoff sniffs at us from the backdoor. I look at my watch. "Hey, man," I say. "Your flight get in early?"

He doesn't move to shake hands. Instead, he tugs at his suit jacket and frowns around the kitchen. "I was expecting more progress on my investment, Donovan."

My brows fly up. "We're on time, which is a miracle considering some of the situations we've worked through."

Kenneth shakes his head. "I give zero shits about situations. I need this place on the market ASAP. How long until it's habitable?"

Chris clears his throat. "I don't want to tell you how to do your job, but there's nothing stopping you from listing the house at this stage."

Kenneth whips his head around. "And you are?"

"This is my foreman." I place a hand on Chris's back, feeling defensive. My jaw is set and my voice drops a few octaves when I say, "Chris, why don't you run through what you were just showing me about the bathrooms and kitchen?"

The very modest budget didn't leave us a lot of space to get the sort of high-end fixtures Kenneth the Jagoff was expecting, and Chris salvaged a lot of materials from a reuse store. The granite countertops were the one big splurge after we got the restaurant-quality kitchen appliances from a going-out-of-business sale.

But the client is not impressed. "People don't want used furniture," he says, practically kicking the massive stainless-steel fridge as he flails.

Chris arches a brow. "The house itself is used... this isn't new construction."

Kenneth flares his nostrils. "I was promised it would look and feel like new. I need this to appeal to luxury buyers. Christ, I should have known better than to go with a janky operation like this. You know what? Just tell your guys to get out of here. I'll have another crew take over."

My jaw hangs open. He's barely spent time in Pittsburgh, not to mention he's disrespecting Dad's crew. I might be lousy at the business side of the business, but I've known most of these guys since I was in braces. I'm seeing red, but Chris comes to my rescue. Again.

"No disrespect, but I think you'd lose more money trying to get a crew to step in and take over rather than let us close out the scope of work. We're a week away from painting walls, and that's absolutely something the homeowner can weigh in on if you want to list this place. How many of these projects have you seen through to completion, if you don't mind me asking?"

Kenneth turns red. He purses his lips. "Get the fuck out of my face," he says to Chris.

I suddenly find my voice. "Hey, that's uncalled for, man. You want us out? You got it." I slap the plywood. "Give us the second payment, and we'll clear out."

IT TAKES another hour for Jagoff to stop screaming and yelling at his lawyer on the phone. Thankfully, I had the union check over the contract before we signed it, so there were clauses in there to protect our paycheck in these kinds of situations.

Still, I hate leaving something undone. This house was supposed to prove I could fill my dad's shoes. Instead, it's just a reminder I can't get much right. Seated in the cab of Chris's truck, I take a swig of the pop he hands me.

"That guy was an asshole," Chris says.

"Yeah, but I'm the idiot who took the job. I should have listened to you. Now we have to hustle to find another project."

Chris takes a sip and taps his fingers on the steering wheel. We're still parked outside the house, which Kenneth locked up. He had people come out and change the locks, like we'd come back in and piss on his walls or something. Actually, I'm not above it.

Chris faces me. "Don't take this the wrong way, kid, but working for you isn't the same as working for your old man. Donny and I had a good thing going."

I swallow a lump in my throat. "And you don't feel good when I'm in charge."

"Don't be like that, Nate. I'm just saying I think we need to take a deep breath and figure out what we want to do next."

I press my forehead to the glass, knowing full well he means he, Sparky, and the crew are going their separate ways, and I have no fucking clue what to do other than beg them to let me tag along.

I finish my pop and squeeze the can, checking around for the bin Chris keeps in his truck for recycling. I toss the can in with a clink. "Thanks for the pop. And the pep talk."

"Ah, come on, Donny. I still love you like you're my own. Why don't we go to the Black Sox game tomorrow? We can think better with a beer and a ballgame."

I make plans to meet him at the stadium and climb into my truck. Which is when I remember I was supposed to help Eden this afternoon and have dinner with her sisters. "Fuck me," I mutter, turning over the engine. "This day just keeps delivering."

I HAUL ass to Garfield and jump up the steps two at a time, bursting into Eden's house to find chaos. I don't see her mom anywhere, but my guess is she caused whatever happened. The Storm sisters have hung rows of string throughout the dining room. There are pans of water bubbling everywhere, the house is a thousand degrees, and it looks like nun chucks are swaying in the breeze of a bunch of oscillating fans.

I spy Eliza pulling nun chucks from a giant pot... no, not weaponry. Candles. I step over to her. "Hey, is Eden here? I'm sorry I'm late."

Eliza's eyes fly wide. "You picked a day, didn't you, Donovan?" Eliza gestures toward the kitchen with a candle. I'll have to remember to ask later why there are two hooked together by one piece of string.

When I step into the kitchen, Eva has her tongue sticking out as she slaps labels on tiny jars while Eden murmurs to herself and fills the jars from a funnel of goo. Everyone is dripping in sweat. I stick my hands in my pocket and wait for one of them to see me. I don't want to interrupt anyone's rhythm.

Eventually, Eden looks up and sets down her goo funnel. "Oh sure, now you show up."

I stumble backward from the venom in her tone and nearly knock over a tower of labeled jars. "I tried to call," I tell her. "I had a work emergency."

Eden snorts and waves around the kitchen as Eva tries to sneak out of the room. "*This* is a work emergency. I was counting on your help today. Or did you forget you made a promise last night?"

"Eden..." I hold my palms up. "I texted you the property owner was flying in today at three. I'm sorry I didn't follow up again this morning, but I thought you would understand that work is a priority."

Eden shoves the goo funnel toward the sink. "You were the one who told me I never make myself a priority. *You* said that. I tried to do that just one time, and what happens? My mother shits on everything she touches, and you don't show up when you say you're going to."

I close my eyes and count to three before I respond. "You're upset. Can we get some ice water and some food in you?" I should have brought food, but I wanted to get here as soon as I could and barely stopped for red lights.

"Upset? *Upset*?" Eden tugs at her hair and stomps her foot. "I had to throw out half the wax. It had fucking dirt in it and smelled like cigarettes. Do you know how much money I'm out because my mother didn't want to put herself on mute during a Zoom call?"

"Where is Emma?" I look around, confused about the order of events here, but Eden's in no place to explain.

"I made her leave," she shrieks. "I had to kick my own mother out of my house. Do you know what that feels like?"

Eliza pokes her head in from the dining room. "I bet it felt cathartic, Eden. You were amazing, babe."

"Shut up!" Eden closes her eyes and digs her fists into her temples. "Everyone just shut up. I can't think right now." She reaches for the funnel, like she's going to keep working. I can see she has a recipe or instructions or something all covered in stains on the table behind her. The mudroom is cluttered with bee frames and rubber bands, wood bits and chunks of wax splattering the floor. It looks exactly how I feel on the inside, and I wish I could tell this to Eden, but she's clearly not in a place to listen.

"Hey," I start. Her eyes whip in my direction. "I'm here now. If you give me marching orders, I can help you clean up."

She shakes her head and tears run down her cheeks, leaving little trails of clean through her dirt-streaked face. I take a step toward her. I can't fuck up my career and my relationship all in one day. But Eden stiffens and steps back away from me.

"I think you should go," she says.

"Let me help you, and we can talk."

Eliza and Eva poke their heads around the corner, and Eden practically growls at them. "Stay out of this."

They back away, hands up in a peace gesture. Eden is so obviously distraught, stressed to the max. I wish she'd let me help her. I take a step forward, but Eden's eyes flash with rage. "Everyone is telling me to set boundaries. Nobody but my sisters has ever shown up for me when it matters, and I am setting a boundary. You didn't show up when I needed you today, and I'm too fucked up to discuss it. This is why I can't have a relationship. I need to focus on my bees. Just go. Please."

I look at her one final time, taking in the gorgeous, capable, sweaty mess of her. There was never a world where she would end up with a construction worker who can't even handle a flip job without it going up in flames. I turn on my heel and leave like she asked.

21

EDEN

"Hey, sis?" Eliza winces from the other room, Eva hiding behind her. They've clearly overheard my tantrum.

I sink to the floor when Nate closes the door behind him, and once the sound of his boots fades away, I cry even harder.

Eliza reaches me first, Eva rushing to my other side. I sniffle into their ponytails as my sisters sit with me on the floor. Eliza makes a clucking sound, and Eva draws back from the group hug.

"Are you using goat noises to comfort our sister?"

I can't help but laugh, although Eliza is indignant. "Comfort is comfort. And look... It worked."

I laugh harder as I use the back of my hand to scrub tears from my cheeks. "I don't know that I feel comforted exactly." I slump to the floor so I'm lying on the hardwood, staring at the ceiling Eila and I painted to mimic a stormy sky.

Eva and Eliza lie on either side of me, glancing at our paint job.

"I don't know that I've ever noticed this ceiling," Eliza says. "It's pretty cool."

"Mom hates it. She added it into her list of reasons the house is *eclectic.*"

"Who the fuck cares what she thinks? Like she's the queen of healthy choices." Eliza shudders. "Honest to God, Eden, I'm glad you tossed her out. It's too damn stressful having her around, seeing all her shit clear as day and realizing we are miracles for surviving her parenting without going to prison."

"Yeah," Eva says, rolling to her side and resting her head on her arm. "I really am sorry I brought her back like that."

I pat my baby sister's arm. "I don't want you to feel guilty. I guess it's a growth opportunity or something. That's what Marsha would say."

As if summoned, Marsha pokes her head in the front door and peers around the chaos to see us sprawled on the floor in the dining room. "Did you just say my name? Where the hell have you been, Eden? You missed Honey Rollers."

I scramble upright and check my watch. "Oh my God, today is Tuesday, isn't it? Marsha, I'm so sorry."

Marsha walks around the house and whistles. Every spare surface either holds boxes of hastily packaged products, equipment to melt and render beeswax, or wire racks to hang candles. Furniture is overturned and scattered, courtesy of Mom's not-so-subtle exit. Marsha stands with her hands on her hips, squinting toward the mudroom where the last batch of wax simmers over the low flame Eliza was tending before I had a tantrum and threw Nate out.

"I take it you haven't been checking your phone," Marsha says, a grin tipping the side of her mouth.

I sigh and stand, wringing my hands together. "I really am sorry. Did Ghita fill in?"

Marsha grunts affirmatively. "Course she did. I'm just checking on you. I've been worried ever since your mother stormed the party." She snorts. "Storm! Get it?"

Eva laughs, but I sniffle, another round of tears threatening to erupt.

"Hey," Marsha soothes. "Want to talk about it? Tell Dr. Shultz." She looks around, presumably for somewhere to sit, but the floor is the only option. So she sinks down and pats the hardwood at her side.

"I'm going to butt out," Eliza gets to her feet. "But whatever you tell Marsha, make sure it includes you going above and beyond to deal with our mother when you absolutely do not owe her a fucking thing."

My stomach roils at those words. Do I really believe I owe my mother... something? I don't actually know. Eliza blows me a kiss and drags Eva into the other room.

The sounds of Eva and Eliza quietly starting to finish things up in the kitchen—hopefully stirring in the measured ingredients from the salve recipe—provide a surprisingly cathartic back track. I groan again, just to feel the vibration in my chest, and unload on Marsha.

"And then Nate was supposed to come help, but I guess a work thing came up, and he said he called but..." I shrug and gesture around. I'm not even sure where my phone is. I bury my face in my hands. I'm the worst. "He was trying to be here for me. He didn't have to agree to come over today to begin with. Who wants to volunteer to help their girlfriend work? I'm such a greedy brat. And now I stood up the Honey Rollers, so I'm a hypocrite, too."

Marsha pulls me in for a hug and holds me while I let out another extended bout of tears.

"You've had a heck of a month," she says into my hair. "It's okay to lose your temper. What's your plan for repair?"

"Repair?" I draw back, my brows knit together.

She tuts. "Yeah. Repair. What you do to make amends after you make a mistake. Sounds like you treated Nate unfairly."

I nod. "I'm a monster. He's having his own awful time, too. I just... wanted someone to rescue me, I think."

Marsha hooks a thumb toward the kitchen. "Someone like those broads?"

"They're always there for me. I wanted... I wanted someone to show up for me who isn't biologically required. It sounds awful when I say it that way."

Marsha is quiet for a few moments, either thinking of what to say next or trying to figure out how to tell me I suck.

"I care about you, kid, and we aren't related," she says, giving my arm a playful pinch. "And I know you never had it easy. You need to find a professional to help you figure out what comes next."

"Like therapy?"

Marsha nods.

"My sister Eila has a therapist. But she also has health insurance and a steady job."

"There are options out there. Want me to send you some stuff?"

I blink, indecision making it hard to form the words I want. Marsha lets me off the hook.

"You have the ability to be whoever you want, Eden. You are a gifted beekeeper, but you're also kind, and you have a lot to offer. Mental health pros can help you make sense of your feelings so they're not holding you back, you know?"

"Holding me back?" I furrow my brow, not used to this kind of conversation with Marsha. She often talks about the psychology of a hive, and I know she works in the mental health arena, but we rarely talk about her work apart from her side hustle hives.

Marsha sighs. "Let's just say you have a lot of great things going for you. You've got your sisters, and you've got the Honey Rollers... when you remember to show up."

I groan, and she gives my shoulder a playful shove.

"I'm messing with you. I know you're an independent woman, and I know you have a real thing going with Nate. I want you to know you have the tools to stick up for yourself with that mother of yours before she turns you into a pressure cooker of stress and you explode all over the people you actually enjoy being around."

I'm tired just thinking about Marsha's words, because they ring so true. I really have taken things out on my sisters and most especially Nate, all because I wasn't brave enough to stand up to my mother sooner. Why is it easier to lash out at the people in my life who are nice to me?

I turn to Marsha, tears blurring my vision. "How do I get started?"

Marsha squeezes my leg. "I'm going to text you a bunch of stuff. You can pick some groups that feel right." There's a clatter in the kitchen, followed by muttered curses. Marsha stands up. "Come on. Let's get your house put together before your bees decide to move in."

22

NATE

FOR THE FIRST time in maybe ever, I have no reason to be out of bed in the morning. There are a million things I need to take care of in terms of paperwork, but I don't have a job site to get to. I don't have a girlfriend to dote on. I have no close family.

I'm just wallowing in the semi-darkness of my room in a bed that still smells like Eden's shampoo from the last time she slept here. I feel pathetic, burying my face in her pillow and inhaling, but I've been pathetic before.

My mind plays Eden's words, Kenneth the Jagoff's words on repeat, a visual of Chris's disappointed face as he drove from the Morningside house for the last time accompanying the soundtrack.

I'm going to have to stop going to my grief group. It'll be too hard to drive by the physical representation of my failure.

The sound of my phone ringing startles me; I thought I turned it off. Honestly, I thought I smashed it last night when I got home from Eden's place. When I answer, Chris yells at me before I can even say hello.

"Are you coming out here, or do I have to come in there and drag you?"

I sit up. "What are you talking about?"

"The game, Donovan. The Black Sox? We're going to go drink shitty beer and have a good wallow while the Sox lose, remember?"

I scratch at my hair, frowning. "Did we say we were doing that?"

Chris grumbles, and then I hear a pounding on my front door. "Come on," he yells, both in real life and through the phone, assaulting my ears with a double bellow.

"All right, give me a minute to pee."

I STUMBLE into some jeans and manage to find a Sox shirt. When I open the front door, Chris thrusts a greasy paper bag in my face. "Donuts," he grunts. "Let's go."

I open the bag and inhale the cinnamon scent of a fresh cake donut. "This was my dad's favorite," I mumble, filled with nostalgia and grief and fondness as I bite into the pastry.

"He ate too many of the damn things, rest his soul." Chris pulls his hand off the gearshift to cross himself as he navigates his truck toward the baseball stadium. "First pitch is at one. We probably won't make it."

I talk around a mouth full of sugar. "Sorry I held us up."

He waves a hand and then snaps on the radio, listening to the pre-game commentary. The Sox haven't had a winning season in decades, but it is nice to go to the games. The stadium sits right along the Allegheny River, near where it merges with the Monongahela to become the Ohio. No matter where you sit, you can see something spectacular, whether it's the skyscrapers downtown or all the bridges on either side of the stadium, connecting all the neighborhoods together despite the massive waterways that would otherwise divide the city.

Chris finds a free parking spot along the river trail, and we walk to the stadium, grabbing cheap bleacher seats along the third baseline and settling in just in time for the first pitch. I nudge him with my shoulder. "Want me to grab us some drinks?"

He shakes his head and hooks his thumb at a guy selling beer in the stands. "Cold IC Lite! Cold beer here," he yells.

I beckon the guy over, grabbing a few cans as Chris smiles approvingly.

We sit in silence for a few minutes, and it really does feel better, watching the Sox get struck out with a cold drink in the warm sun. Between innings, Chris turns sideways in the bleachers to face me.

"So..." he says, then he waits.

I sigh. "I'm sorry, man. I tried really hard to run things like my dad did, but I am not cut out to run the business. I shouldn't have strung the crew along like I did when I knew it was a sinking ship."

Chris frowns. "Is that what you think? That you sunk

us?" He swallows. "You were never late with a paycheck. And you aren't the first person to have some out-of-state asshole throw a tantrum and cancel a job. The number of times your old man called me to bitch about that exact thing..." He crumples his empty can and sets it on the stands between his legs. "It's not that you're bad at it, kid. We can see you hate it."

I let that sink in for a bit, wincing. "Is it that obvious?"

"I knew from the moment you showed up drunk at that Squirrel Hill reno that you were not living your best life, Donny."

I know he's bringing up a major mistake I made, but it feels so good to hear him use his nickname for my father... on me.

"I really do like doing the work, though," I say. "I'm good at building things. Just not..." I wave my hands around. "Payroll and insurance and union dues. Who likes that kind of stuff? It's awful. You know, my girlfriend applied for an entire USDA grant in the time it took me to reconcile my books? I had to learn the word reconcile."

Chris shoots an arm out toward a food vendor and soon hands me half of a cold, salty pretzel. He takes a huge bite of his, talking around it. "Donny would never want you to be miserable, kid."

I take a tentative bite of my pretzel, aware I've only eaten junk food so far today, which is apparently the recipe for soothing big feelings. "Who says I'm miserable?"

Chris ruffles my hair like I'm still a teenager. "Nate, I knew your old man my whole life." His eyes are wet as he chews another bite of the terrible pretzel. "You were his whole world. The business? He built it for you."

I throw the rest of my pretzel on the ground between my feet. "I know that. Why do you think I'm twisting myself around trying to fix it?"

He shakes his head. "You're missing my point. He built it for you, so you'd have something if you need it. But you've got your own things. Maybe what you really need is space." He shrugs. "I'm just saying, Donny wouldn't want you to be miserable, and it's plain to see you are. I said what I said."

I watch the game in silence for a few pitches to let it sink in. He's right. They've all been right—my group, Eden, Chris... It's my own damn head that's been so stubborn.

"What do I do instead?" I ask him.

He guffaws and gestures around the stadium, toward the river. "Buy a boat. Drive a school bus. Whatever the hell you want, kid."

I cross my arms, elbows touching Chris and the guy sitting on my other side. "I like building shit, Chris. I'm just not cut out to be in charge."

He shakes his head at the umpire, or maybe me, or maybe both. By the third inning, we've agreed that Sparky would be a great candidate to run the show. I hope he'll agree to hire me on his crew, since I'm going out of business and need to find a job.

WE DRINK a second round of lite beer and are waiting for the Sox to take the field when we hear terrified screams from the outfield fence a few hundred feet to our left. Chris takes a swig of his drink, watching as people flee the stands. "What the hell is all that about?" He points with his can, and I squint just as the cameras pan on the situation, putting the scene on the jumbotron.

It's a familiar sight—a formation Eden calls a beard. Thousands of bees have swarmed on the wall that display the scores of the other games being played around the league. The backup pitchers hustle out of the nearby bullpen. Stadium staff doesn't seem to know what to do.

"Is that a bee nest?" Chris squints at the wall on the riverside of the outfield.

We head down the bleachers to the rail above the field. Most of the people in our section have left, and I lean forward just in time to see the ground crew sprint onto the grass.

"Hey!" I shout to one of the guys before I can think better of the idea. He turns his head, and I wave him over. "I know someone who can fix this," I tell him. "I know a beekeeper."

23

EDEN

.

"EDEN? I brought scones! Are you in there?" Esther's voice floats up the stairs, pulling me from sleep. I'm not sure how long I stayed up with Marsha and my sisters. At one point Marsha suggested I eat a teaspoon of "funny honey"—blended with THC—and I passed out on the couch.

I crack open one eye, my oldest sister strolling into my house. Did I give her a spare key or did I fall asleep without locking the door? I sure hope it was the first option, because the last thing I want is to start a habit that will lead my mother to invade.

Esther drops a bag on the coffee table, puts her hands on her hips, and glances around. The candles are still hanging all over the first floor. In place of the dirty equipment and piles of beeswax shavings, there are neatly stacked rows of labeled jars. My Storm Swarm products are ready to box up and deliver.

"You've been busy," Esther says, plopping down beside me. "Who will take all the candles?"

I cover a yawn. "There's a gift shop in Oakland. Another one at the conservatory."

Esther runs a finger along a row of candle pairs dangling from their shared wick. "Can I buy a batch for the bar? These are classy."

"What? You stopped shaving the stickers off reused prayer candles?"

Esther shrugs. "We are all always doing a little better than the day before, right?"

I reach for the bag and pull out scones from the bakery down the hill. "Oh, shit, these are fresh," I sigh, sinking my teeth into the sweet, nutty delight.

Esther sips from a to-go coffee and waits for me to take a few bites before she says, "Sooo... the girls called me."

I pause with a scone midway to my mouth, my hand hovering in the air as I clench for Esther to give me a stern lecture.

Instead, she squeezes my leg. "I'm really proud of you for kicking Mom out. I know that wasn't easy."

I sink into the couch in relief, the muscles in my legs loosening along with the tension in my guts. I didn't know I needed her to praise me like that. "Okay, so I'm a mess and I messed up. What do I do next?"

Esther leans back, shoulder pressing into mine. "I hear a *lot* of stories from a *lot* of fucked up people. It wouldn't hurt any of us to get some help. The Storm sisters, I mean."

The enormity of her revelation pulses through me like someone struck a gong. My big sister, who held us all together, is placing herself beside me in this idea that something is wrong, and there's maybe a way to fix it. I swallow the last dry bit of scone, choke, and reach for Esther's coffee. Then I cough more because I forgot she drinks it black. Once I have myself together, I say, "Marsha was going to send me some resources. Mental health stuff that's affordable." I bite my lip and look around. "I'd really like to check it out. It would mean a lot if you came with me."

Esther gestures for her coffee. "I can't promise I'll get chatty."

I nod and pop my lips a few times before I say, "I was thinking maybe all of us could go. Like as a family."

Esther wrinkles her nose, considering. "Huh. Well, I definitely think it would be good for Eva. Who even knows if Eliza will talk to humans."

We finish our breakfast on the couch, and I'm about to stand up and start boxing the candles when the front door flies open. Eva bursts inside, waving her phone around. "Oh my God, Eden, turn on the TV." She halts in the living room, like she suddenly remember that I don't own a television. She growl and taps around on her phone. "Look."

She shoves her screen in my face. There's a sports field and a lot of people running around screaming in a way that's become familiar to me. "Is that—?"

The announcer's voice comes through the microphone, tinny and frantic. "That's right, folks. There is a swarm of bees infesting the outfield scoreboard here in Pittsburgh. It's pandemonium on the field as the Black Sox and Dragons have retreated to their locker rooms. Fans are—"

Eva drops the phone, and the sound goes off, but Esther is already on her feet. "Eden," she says. "This is your moment."

I frown. "My moment for what?"

Eva grins. "To get your name out there as the best beekeeper in the land. Go save the park!"

I groan. "First of all, the park is fine. My concern is with those tiny gals who are clearly looking for a cool, comfortable place to brood their babies."

"Okay, fine," Eva says, stomping her foot. "Get up and go save the babies."

My face contorts in confusion. "Eva. I don't know people at the ballpark. I can't just show up and tell them I'm a beekeeper to the rescue. Who do I even tell? The gate attendant?"

She's about to argue when my phone rings somewhere in the dining room. Esther steps away to find it, and I hear her grunting and growling, moving things around. The phone stops ringing and immediately starts again, and Esther must finally find it because she yells, "Hello! This is the beekeeper's helper!"

Eva and I dart into the dining room, a cacophony drifting from my phone. Esther holds it a foot away from her face as a man howls about being the groundskeeper at the Black Sox stadium, in desperate need of my services. "Some guy named Nate Donovan swears you can help us."

I gasp. Would Nate make this sort of connection for me after everything I said? I stare at Esther, who holds the phone out to me. "But I was so mean to him," I whisper. Esther snatches the phone back.

"Eden Storm will be at the stadium in fifteen minutes. Where should we have her enter, and who should we ask for?"

TWELVE MINUTES LATER, Esther slams on the brakes in my van, causing Eva and all the supplies to shift around in the back. I pop the veil on my head as Eva bursts from the van with my temporary hive and frames, which she shoves at me.

Men in coveralls wave their arms frantically, spotting me in my white bee kit. I don't normally wear the suit, but I wasn't sure how angry these bees would be after all those people ran around them screaming. Plus, Eva insisted this gives me more credibility.

"Everyone trusts someone in a uniform," she said before stuffing me into my seat in the van.

Amidst the chaos, Esther grabs my smoker and pulls a lighter from her back pocket. She opens the top and ignites the twigs and pine needles before shoving the whole thing toward Nate, who has materialized out of nowhere. My heart skips a beat, like I'm in a romance movie. I want to rush toward him and tell him how very sorry I am for my outburst yesterday. But he's standing there alongside a guy I sort of recognize from his construction crew, and there are bees in peril.

A flustered groundskeeper—Eva is right, uniforms really help with identification—runs up to me and doesn't even speak. He gestures toward a waiting golf cart, and I follow him, Nate hot on my tail with the smoker.

The second the cart zooms onto the field, the remaining crowd bursts into cheers. I allow myself to soak in their applause. I love helping—this is what I love about my job, second only to interacting with the bees. When the golf cart stops, I set my things on the grass, and then the groundskeeper speeds away faster than I ever thought those things could go.

But Nate hasn't left. He's there, with a metal smoker. He grins at me and holds out a queen clip. "Need a hand?"

24

NATE

EVEN THOUGH EDEN is dressed head to toe in white canvas and a veil, she's hot as hell doing her thing with the bees in the outfield. I watch from a distance as she strides over to them, talking to them, telling them she's here to help. I swear, they hear her. It's like the whole swarm parts when she extends her hand to search for the queen.

The stadium erupts in oohs and ahhs, and a drone camera flies right over her head, televising her work. It's not long before the announcer says something about the mysterious beekeeper to the rescue. I wish I could get someone over here to give them Eden's information to share, but it seems more important to stay close by and help her if she needs me.

A few minutes pass, and Eden turns, a triumphant grin beaming through her veil as she holds up the clip.

"You got the queen?" I set the bee box on the ground and hope blooms in my chest. It's got to mean something that she brought the box I made her, for a big, public bee rescue.

Eden clips the queen to one of the frames, and just like she always promises, most of the bees follow within a few minutes. Eden takes the smoker and coaxes the rest along. She sets up some of the frames and rubber bands in the box and when the scene is clear, she plucks off a single piece of honeycomb the swarm put together between innings.

When Eden puts the lid on the box, the stadium erupts in cheers. The crowd has mostly filed back to their seats, curious to watch Eden's work. I'm worried the park is going to set off the outfield home-run fireworks before we clear the area, but thankfully, they don't.

The grounds crew is still AWOL, so Eden struggles with the box while I walk at her side, carrying her gear. I guess they're going to just watch us make our way across the entire outfield, infield, and through the tunnel where we came in.

Eden blushes at all the applause, pink cheeks just visible through her bee veil. Once it's clear we have the situation in hand, a camera operator scurries toward us, a reporter and microphone holder in hot pursuit.

"That was amazing," the reporter exclaims, tugging at the neck of his polo shirt. Eden grins.

The reporter gestures toward the box of bees. A few fly around the handles that serve as entry and exit doors for the little critters. The reporter tries to get close enough to mic Eden but is obviously frightened of all the buzzing. "What are you going to do with them?"

Eden shifts the weight of the box. "Well, I'll take them home and quarantine the hive until I'm sure they're all healthy. Then I'll incorporate them into the fold. I can build a new permanent hive for them alongside my others."

The reporter takes a tentative step closer to Eden. "And will this new hive be black and gold for the Sox?" He flashes his teeth in a fake-television smile, but Eden shakes her head. "Black would be way too hot for these guys. But maybe I can paint a little logo on the lid." She laughs uncomfortably. I can see sweat forming on Eden's forehead. She's still wearing the veil and struggling under the weight of the box.

Once it's clear nobody is going to help carry it, I set down the smoker and gesture for the box. Eden's eyes fly wide. The reporter is bouncing with excitement and turns to face me. "And who is this?"

I grab the box from Eden, who immediately pulls off her veil and fans herself with it. "Since you didn't ask, *this* is Eden Storm, of Storm Swarm. You should look for her honey and beeswax products at restaurants and gift shops all around the city."

The reporter turns to the cameras. "Did you hear that, folks? Eden Storm is going to take these bees out of this ballpark and make magic. Wouldn't we all like a little Black Sox special soap to wash up after we sweated over this situation?"

The crowd titters with laughter. I grunt and head toward the tunnel, and Eden walks behind me, her white suit swishing with every step.

Once we're in the service entrance, I set down the box and turn to face Eden.

"Hey," I say.

A full stadium has never been so silent. There is

nothing but this tunnel and the two of us. Well, and one million of her bee friends, but they're rooting for us. I know it.

She unzips her suit and lets it fall open like a banana peel, slithering off her shoulders. She steps out of the pants. "Hey," she whispers. And then she starts to cry.

I wrap her in my arms, inhaling the smoky scent of her work over her signature honeysuckle and spice. "Eden, sweetheart, I'm here, okay? I know you told me to forget you, but that's never going to happen."

"Ughhh," she moans into my shirt. "I don't deserve you being nice to me like this."

I shake my head. "Don't say that. You are everything good and loving and caring, and people have shit all over you. I get that. I let you down the other day. I've been letting a lot of people down. But I'm working hard to change that. And I wanted you to know I'm always thinking of you."

Eden lets out a whimper and hugs me tight. I pat her hair, wishing we could go somewhere more private to continue this conversation. When I look up, the groundskeeping staff are all standing around us in a circle. Someone in a suit is stumbling toward Eden, red-faced.

"Ms. Storm?" the suit guy asks. "Can I have a word?"

I drape an arm around her shoulder as she turns in my arms to face him. "Sure," she says, eyes flicking to the box of bees on the ground in the shade. The box is humming with activity, and I know from experience there is a magical transformation happening inside. I think about how those little critters burrowed inside a dirty, crumbling wall, and Eden managed to coax them out alongside gallons of sweetness people will be enjoying for a long time.

It's hopeful, is what it is.

The guy in the suit clears his throat. "I'm Ted Bascoe, owner of the Pittsburgh Black Sox. I'd like to thank you personally for your intervention today so that we can continue the game." He pauses at the crack of a bat hitting a ball, and a crowd roars in delight. "I'm not sure what fee was discussed, but I'd like to offer you a gratuity. Do you have a card so I can contact your admin to set up a meeting to discuss the Black Sox Stadium Soap you mentioned to the reporter?"

Eden blinks a few times. I know damn well nobody discussed a fee with her because I was there when Joe from the grounds crew hollered for her to get here immediately. I'm just glad she was near her phone.

"Hey," I say, while Eden coughs and wriggles. "Can she get a bottle of water?"

An hour later, I climb inside the passenger seat of Eden's van, reminding myself I don't need to be afraid of the bees in the back. She handed me her veil to put on if I got super uncomfortable, but I just spin it in my hands as she puts the van in gear and navigates onto Route 28 toward her house.

"So," she says, merging onto the highway, "I'm really sorry I shut you out. I totally lost my shit, like everything from the past month piled up until I exploded."

I flip the veil, staring at the fabric. "I'm really sorry you had to deal with so much stress."

She turns briefly before snapping her eyes to the road. "You're under a ton of stress, too, though, and you're not screaming or yelling or accusing anyone of anything."

"No," I agree. "I'm more prone to self-destruct and make terrible choices."

She grunts.

"I used to think the only person I was hurting was me when I acted that way. Like who the hell cared if I was drunk and dumb?"

She bites her lip. "What changed?"

"You left me a furious voicemail, and I realized I don't live in a vacuum." I turn to face the buzzing box in the back. "I'm part of a hive, even if I don't realize it."

"That seems right." Eden takes a deep breath. "I shouldn't treat you that way. I want you to know I have a plan to work on it. On myself. And my feelings and stuff."

I smile and settle more comfortably into the chair. "That's good to hear." Now it's my turn to take a deep breath. "I'm selling the business. We lost the contract on the Morningside house. I'm not too good at the management side of construction."

"Oh, Nate, that's not true! We can work together and—"

I hold up a hand. "I don't like doing it. I talked it through with my grief group, and Chris and I had a really long talk today before the game went up in smoke."

She laughs. "Oh… did we grab my smoker?"

"I dumped out the insides, too, like you had shown me."

She moans in relief. I try not to let the sound turn me on. "You are really good at helping me."

"Thank you. I'll have a little more time for that... if you want me around." I tap my fingers on the veil. "I'm about to be unemployed."

Eden taps the steering wheel a few times. "Maybe I could hire you to build me some things. For my business."

I reach for her hand, squeezing it gently. "That sounds amazing."

25

EDEN

TWO MONTHS LATER

I give my computer screen a gentle pat. I just made sales projections. *Projections!* This is a word I use now.

I turned Eila's bedroom into an office, set up a real computer, took some seminars at the agricultural extension program, and mapped out plans for each quarter and goals for five years. I'm basically an adult now.

"Hey, babe, can you come take a look at these valves?" Nate's voice carries up the stairs from the kitchen. Initially, I hired him on a job-by-job basis, but he kept having more ideas for custom hives and frames and beekeeping supplies and... Well, we set up an online store. Who knew beekeepers from all over the world would be interested in Storm Swarm products?

"Coming!" I click save on my sales projections report and hurry down the stairs to find my hunky boyfriend bent over a brand-new extractor he's been working on. I take a few beats to admire the view. "What am I looking at?"

He turns over one shoulder to smile at me and tips his head, beckoning for me to come closer.

I run a hand along the stainless-steel drum. "It's so shiny. I love it."

Nate chuckles. "That's not even the good part. Look here."

I peer between his strong hands to see the innards of a honey release valve at the bottom of the machine. I can put a huge bucket down there or—depending what I'm bottling—a tiny jar.

"And I won't even have to plug it up with wax when I'm between vessels." I clap my hands. "Nate, it's perfect. Thank you." I drop a kiss to the nape of his neck and stand back to watch as he finishes his work. He pauses frequently to take notes on a tiny notebook I swear he got from my sister Esther, who also writes her ideas by hand when she's designing.

I take a minute to appreciate the ways my boyfriend is similar to my oldest sister—two people I admire, who take care of me and let me love them back.

Nate's forearms flex as he tightens something and then he rocks on his heels. "I like it. Are we able to do a test run later? Maybe from the hive at my house?"

I click my tongue, thinking, and check the calendar on my phone. "Oh," I mutter. "I have group later."

Nate peeks at my calendar, and I hold the phone out so he can see. "Right. Hm, I could always drive to Marsha or Muriel and see if one of them has a frame or two I can test. I really want to finalize this so I can get going on the easy-flow hive I'm building for Devesh."

Two months ago, this conversation would have

stressed me out. I would have crammed down my discomfort and told Nate I could grab my own frame rather than potentially overwhelm Marsha with a request.

But I'm eight weeks into a study in the psychology department at Pittsburgh University, and my group has been working on communication and naming emotions. Marsha sent me the info for the researcher, who mostly works with teens and young adults, and I just made the age cutoff. So did Eva. Nobody was surprised when Eliza said she didn't want to talk to humans.

I take a deep breath. "I'd definitely want to check with Marsha or Muriel before driving over there. Is there a way to work on Devesh's project before your test for this one?"

Nate scratches his chin and pulls out his own calendar. He's been using some digital tools to help him manage his time, and he says the paperwork is less terrible when it's for a project he came up with. He pops his lips. "Would you feel comfortable with me grabbing a frame from the hive and testing?"

"Oh," I say, leaning against the counter. "Wow." Nate has been very hands on with me ever since the baseball stadium swarm, but he's never opened a hive on his own. I try to decide if I trust him to do that, but it doesn't take me long to answer. "Yeah, babe. If you feel ready, I think that's a great idea."

He steps into my space, the corner of his mouth lifting. "I don't know how anyone ever feels ready to reach into a beehive. But watching you do it every day gives me confidence."

I inch my legs farther apart to let him settle in. "That's such a nice thing to say."

"I can be nice." He presses a toe-curling kiss to my neck. "And you're very sweet."

He takes the phone from my hand and puts both our devices on the counter before wrapping his arms around me. I sink into his embrace and return his kisses, loving how much fun my work is alongside Nate. I thought it would be weird, working with someone I'm dating, but we have a great rhythm going. We even have staff meetings once a week to study the weather and write our project plans on the whiteboard in the dining room.

These little morale breaks are a nice bonus.

"Oh, my," I squeak as Nate's fingers tickle down the back of my shorts.

He pinches my backside and grins. "We've got… fifteen minutes before you have to leave?"

I drop my head against the cupboard to give him access to my neck, which he licks. And then he keeps licking his way to the collar of my tank top.

"Yes," I gasp. "Fifteen… minutes." My tank is up and over my head in a flash, and Nate rolls up my sports bra.

Once my boobs are bared, he massages them with rough palms. The contrast between his skin and his tongue trailing along behind makes me dizzy, and I swoon as he nibbles one nipple. "Let me get you up on the counter," he says, lifting me with a gentle huff. I rock back as he opens my shorts and awkwardly strips them from my body, dangling them over the rim of my new honey extractor.

And then Nate is on his knees on the kitchen floor,

grinning up at me from his blond lashes as he spreads my thighs. I scoot to the edge of the counter, deciding to stop worrying about time when his tongue brushes along my seam.

"Mmm," he moans, and I drop a hand into his hair. He's a little sweaty and a lot sexy as he peers up at me, licking his lips. "You've got some honey for me, Eden?"

A gasp slips through my teeth as he runs a finger through my wetness. My body responds to him so dramatically. He has learned exactly how to make me feel good, over and over again. We've practiced in the garden, in the kitchen, among the hives. Now that it's autumn, I've really enjoyed cuddling with him under blankets on the cracked leather couch at his house.

"Oh!" I gasp as Nate slides two fingers inside me, pressing his thumb to my clit. He leans in to kiss my stomach, my upper thighs. He kisses all over as he strokes and presses. When he moves his tongue back to my center, I come.

My body shudders and jerks on the counter as he licks at me, stroking and applying gentle pressure on my clit to help me ease down from the super sensitive aftershocks of my orgasm. When I can breathe again, I remove my hand from his hair. "Oh, Nate, did I pull? I'm so sorry."

I massage his scalp, and he shakes his head.

"You were perfect, Eden. It's amazing watching you." He shifts his weight and starts to stand, reaching behind him for my shirt.

"Wait." I clasp his hand. "What about you?"

He boxes me in against the counter, nestling between

my naked thighs, framing my torso with his powerful arms against the cabinets. "I love making *you* feel good."

I lock my ankles behind him, digging my booted heels into his butt for emphasis. "What if I want more feeling good? From this guy." I jut my hips against the hard bulge in his pants. Sometimes Nate gets me off and then walks around half hard all day. "Can you be fast?"

He laughs and unzips his fly. "Babe. I can be so fast." He pulls out his cock, and I latch onto it, stroking along with him. I find a drop of precum at his tip and swirl it around, enjoying the sensation of the warm liquid. I guide him toward my center and scoot even closer to the edge, knowing he will support my weight.

The angle is uncomfortable with my tailbone digging into the counter, but when he slides inside me bare, I forget to care. We went together to a health clinic a month ago for a battery of tests and an IUD. The slide of him now, nothing between us, is like the ultimate collaboration.

"Yes," I hiss, matching his groans. His breath is hot on my cheeks as his hips move.

"Oh, fuck, Eden, you feel so good." He thrusts short and fast, his hands on my butt as he leans back to watch the place where we are connected. "So perfect, babe. God, yes."

I glance down, smiling at what he sees. I grab his face and kiss him, needing him to know that this is everything to me.

"I love you," I whisper, not for the first time, but every time I say it, I feel like it's new. "I love you so much."

"Love you," he grunts in between kisses and thrusts.

"Fucking love this." I know he wants to hold off until I come again, but I also know I'm going to need a little more friction to get there. I slide a hand between us and stroke myself with two fingers as he watches.

"Oh, fuck, Eden. Oh God." His head drops back. The corded muscles in his neck stand out as he tries to wait for me.

"I'm so close, Nate. Look how hot we are together."

He pries his eyes open, and I lock his gaze, my fingers flying on my clit until...

"Yes. Yes, *now*," I moan, coming apart he swells impossibly large. The tip of his dick bumps against something deep inside me, and he squeezes his eyes shut, body quaking as he detonates inside me, pulsing and groaning my name. Our bodies shudder together, and he stills in my arms, head on my shoulder, hands pulling me tight against him.

This is messy and awkward, and we both worked so hard to get here, sweaty and collaborating for pleasure and business and every aspect of our lives.

"I love you," I whisper again. He whispers it back, and then I sigh. "But I need you to pull out so I can go to group therapy."

26

NATE

After Eden leaves for her appointment, I clean the kitchen counters and psych myself up to reach into a beehive in the backyard. I'm no charmer like my girl-friend, so I zip into the extra-large coveralls I ordered once I decided I'm all in for the Storm Swarm company... and its owner.

I pull on my work gloves, slide the veil over my head, and march into the backyard. "Right," I address the bees, who Eden assures me are always listening. "I'm just going to check on you gals and take one of the frames, okay? I have a fresh one for you."

I grab the hive tool and use it to pry open the lid. I can hear the hum of the work inside and there is so much movement, so much collaboration inside. Eden tells me each bee has a job to do—a specific assignment to help the group. I used to wonder what would happen if one of them hated their job or felt like they inherited work that didn't fit them. But Eden says they shift roles depending on what the community needs.

I sense an affinity with them now. "Hey, guys," I whisper, sweating despite the autumn chill. "I'm going to pull out this frame now, okay?" I hold my breath as I lift the wood. It sticks a bit, but then slides up easily in my grasp. I quickly fill the gap with an empty frame I made with wood Sparky salvaged from an old barn.

I lower the lid to the hive and trot to the house with my prize, feeling proud enough to snap a selfie of me with the honey-heavy frame. I send it to Chris and Sparky, who both think I'm nuts to lend my woodworking skills to tiny creatures with stingers. I was doing some odd jobs for them, but lately I've been busy with custom builds for Storm Swarm. I ignore their teasing and slide the frame into the drum of the extractor.

Everything I assembled worked just like I imagined. Pride swells in my chest, alongside a twinge of grief. I'd love for Dad to see this—the beauty of the spinning centrifuge, the slow slosh of the honey gathering in the bottom. I grab an empty jar and line it up under the valve. I could put the stand under there, but I want to hold it, and I delight in the warmth of the honey filling the jar when I open the switch.

Satisfied and excited, I sit at the table, holding the jar of amber liquid. I grab a spoon from a drawer and taste, a moan escaping my lips at the tangy sweetness. A clatter outside pulls me from my nirvana. The mail carrier flicks a set of letters in the flap at the front door. Every day, I feel for the guy who has to not only climb around the hills of Garfield, but also has to trudge up and down the steps of each house.

There's a postcard from Emma, and I try not to growl

at it. Looks like she has taken a job on a cruise ship, which at least means she'll be out at sea and away from Eden and her sisters.

I frown at one of the letters, addressed to both Eden and Eila. It's stamped from a property management company, and I pull out my phone to check the time. Eden should be done with her appointment by now, so I call her up.

"Hey," I say when she answers with a smile in her voice. "Real quick—a letter came and I think it's about the lease on your house. Okay if I open it?"

"Oh. That's weird." She sounds like she's climbing into her van. "Sure, tell me what it says."

There's a pause while I rip open the envelope and Eden tells me she did a lot of listening at therapy today. Some weeks are like that for me in my grief group. I pull out a piece of cream-colored paper and scan it.

"Oh, shit," I mutter. "Your landlord is selling the house."

"What?" Eden sounds pissed. "Can he do that?"

"Well, yeah," I explain. "He owns it and doesn't want to anymore." I think of out-of-state Kenneth buying up houses to flip. Those kinds of guys sometimes buy up a bunch of property and rent it as absentee landlords. I have to figure Eden has one of those, since she never mentions him. I can't imagine he's heavily involved in the property, given all the bees and urban agriculture going on.

An idea occurs to me. "How far away are you?"

I tell Eden I have a plan forming, and as soon as she gets home, I'll spoon-feed her fresh honey and explain it to her. The truth is, I have a long-term plan for Eden and me. I think she's on the same wavelength, and while this is faster than I would have wanted to move on it, this housing situation is a push in the right direction.

Ten minutes later, Eden bursts in the door, frazzled. "I was really feeling like I had my shit together," she says. "I made sales projections. I file my taxes. I have a hot hunk of an employee. But now I'm going to be homeless. And God, my sister's hops are next door. What landlord is going to agree to me having beehives here? This is a disaster."

Eden sinks into a chair in the kitchen. As promised, I hand her a spoonful of the amber honey.

"Oh, Nate..." she squeals. "You did it! I'm sorry. I'm over here complaining about my thing, and you did something really cool."

I set two glasses of water on the table. "Your thing is important, too. But yeah, I did what you do. I talked to them, I took the frame, I replaced the frame... I didn't get stung."

She beams with the spoon in her adorable mouth. "That's so great." She takes one more lick and a sip of water. "Okay, what are you thinking about the house?"

I rest my palms on the table. "What if I buy it?"

She blinks. "You?"

I shrug. "Yeah. I've got money from selling the business. And my dad said real estate is always a good investment. Not that he ever took his own advice."

Eden frowns. "I don't know if I want you to be my landlord."

"You're my boss. What's the difference?"

She purses her lips. "I don't know. It just seems different."

I reach for her hand, desperate to share my idea, see if she's on board. "What if I was your husband instead?"

Her eyebrows fly up. "Husband?"

I kneel on the kitchen floor, pulling her hand into mine. "I was wondering if you'd consider marrying me, Eden Storm."

She stares at me, so I continue. "You make me a better man, Eden. You inspire me and push me to be my best. I love that about you, and I want you to know I'm all in. Forever."

"Forever." Eden squeezes my hand, a tear forming in the corner of her eye. "I like how that sounds, Nate."

I adjust my weight. It's getting a little uncomfortable down here, and she still hasn't given me a proper answer. I raise my brows expectantly. "So will you? Marry me?"

She grabs my cheeks and pulls my face into hers, kissing me. "Yes," she giggles into my mouth. "Yes, Nate Donovan, I will marry you."

I stand, tugging her to her feet and lifting her up, spinning her around. "Everything that's mine will be yours, too, you know. This house. The other house. All of it. This is forever for me."

Eden stares at me, and I squeeze her hands. "Gut reaction," I say. "What are you thinking?"

Her mouth drops open, and she takes a deep breath. "I was thinking... this house could be Storm Swarm Headquarters. The living room has space to package and label and really ramp up honey processing. The dining room could be your workshop." She takes in the tools piled on the built-in bookshelves in the room. "It sort of already is."

"I love that idea. We'd have to talk to Ben about zoning."

She nods. "He loves talking about zoning."

I lean forward. "And I love talking about you."

"Are we really going to get married?"

I nod and pull her into my lap. "As soon as you say the word."

Eden wrinkles her nose. "Do we have to plan a whole big thing? Esther just got married at the courthouse."

I shrug. "So we get married at the courthouse. Or the backyard. I don't care about that part. I'm here for the long haul." I kiss her forehead. "I love you. And I can't wait for you to live with me."

"I love you, too," she says. "I think we make a good team."

EPILOGUE
ELIZA

EVEN I CAN ADMIT the yard looks perfect. Eden was gracious enough to hire one of my goat teams to clear the knotweed from the side lot, and Eva hung fairy lights among the hops plants and set up picnic tables until the entire scene could feature on a Hallmark movie. Very romantic.

My sisters roam around the yard with their various boyfriends and Eden's bee friends, the Honey Rollers. I promised I wouldn't pass out business cards or otherwise be pushy about my goatscaping business, so I'm parked on a bench with a fruity seltzer.

Eden waffled about telling our mom about the wedding, and we all encouraged her it was okay not to mention it. Mom isn't here for any of our yuck, and we don't need to invite her into our yay. Or something like that.

I smile at Nate shaking hands with his construction pals. Nate looks pretty nice in a button-down with suspenders and slacks. I realize Eden hasn't shown me her dress, and I can't decide if I should be insulted. But maybe that's what she was calling about the other week when I was out wrangling ruminants from the South Side Slopes. That was a good contract with the city. Very lucrative.

Esther appears on the back porch of the house. "Hey, everyone…"

There aren't too many of us, but my brother-in-law never misses an opportunity to whistle with his fingers. Esther gets all swoony when Koa puts his thumb and forefinger to his lips, and I try not to gag.

Esther grins. "Eden is about ready, so let's all take our seats."

My family crams onto the benches of the picnic tables, and Eden's friend Marsha taps a microphone she brought along for her role as officiant. Apparently, Marsha got ordained online just for the occasion.

I laugh when Marsha plays Tom Petty's "Honeybee," which is sexy enough that Nate's work friends actually blush behind their beards. But then Eden appears with her dark hair braided into a crown, wildflowers tucked into the plaits. Her dress is a cheerful lemon yellow—I guess it's more accurate to say *honey*-colored—and it falls to her mid-calf. She's barefoot beneath the ruffled skirt, and she holds a bouquet Eila put together for her with goldenrod, witch hazel, and purple asters.

My goats, penned in the back with the last of the knotweed, start to bleat, probably sniffing Eden's flowers. I shush them as my sister makes her way to her beau. Marsha smiles as Eden hands her bouquet to Eila, who sits back down, and then Eden clasps Nate's hands.

"All right, folks," Marsha says, her Minnesota accent adding a layer of charm to this already sweet backyard ceremony. "We're gonna keep this short and simple."

I'm distracted by my goats, who are increasingly agitated as Nate and Eden promise to look after one another and work on building patience and setting healthy boundaries. I stand to try to calm my critters before their guard donkey starts braying and ruining everything.

Just as I approach the pen, Chiron lets out a mighty wail and charges through the chicken wire. I look back in horror as Nate pulls Eden into his arms for a kiss. Ursula, my cranky nanny goat, butts Eden in the butt, pushing her closer to Nate, who just deepens the kiss as everyone laughs.

My face turns red, and I spew apologies. Just what I need, to ruin my sister's wedding with my unruly goats.

But Eden turns around, beaming, petting the black and white goat named for the sea witch. "We did it!" Eden shouts, and all the human guests cheer. I grab Ursula's collar to take her back to the pen, but I miss Cruella, who tears off down Kincaid Street toward Lord knows where. As I take off jogging in my sundress, I hear Eden telling everyone she thinks her wedding was perfect.

I guess some people have different standards.

When I return, goat in tow, the guests are stuffing their faces and debating going bowling. At least I don't have to wait around for a bouquet toss and an awkward promise that I'll be next. I tie the goats, grab a plate of barbecue, and take a seat next to Eva.

She knocks shoulders with me. "See how happy they are," she whispers, pointing her fork at the newlyweds.

She's right. Eden is glowing, and not just from the beeswax candles. Eila clasps hands with Ben, and Esther is draped all over Koa. My sisters seem to have found their place in this world and claimed happiness despite it all.

And I'm happy being the goat lady on the hill. I'm keeping things weird and living alone. Well... Alone apart from my goats. And a very agitated donkey.

As if I summoned him, Chiron brays, which Eden takes as a sign to kiss Nate on the mouth in front of everyone. And they all cheer. But I know why Chiron is actually howling, so I wander over to him with a sprig of goldenrod.

"Here you go, buddy," I say, patting him in between the ears. He licks my cheek, and I smile. This right here is enough. Everything is fine.

Thanks for reading Eden and Nate's story! Continue the Planted and Plowed series with Eliza's book, Yule Be Sorry.

Want more of Eden and Nate? My newsletter subscribers get a steamy bonus scene. Visit LaineyDavis.com to sign up or scan the QR code below.

AUTHOR'S NOTE

Sometimes I have really weird ideas, and then I get to dive into other worlds to turn these wacky ideas into books.

I owe so much to the beekeepers who helped me with this project! Any bee mistakes you see in here are entirely my fault. But please know I had excellent guidance and crammed myself into a white bee suit and put my face right alongside a few different hives full of bees. Actual bees.

Marcia and Heidi were so generous with their expertise and their colonies and my many, many questions.

I'm also indebted to my co-authors from the Farm 2 Forking series, who taught me new ways to draft a book and new ways to seek editorial support. Liz Alden and Karen Grey even took the time to read a very early draft and offer invaluable feedback.

My local author support team is an amazing resource and I'm always blown away by the wisdom of Elizabeth Perry and Melissa Wiesner.

And you, readers, have stuck with me through so many series. I am really excited about the Storm Sisters and I hope you'll hang out for Eliza's book. If you need me, I'll be out and about visiting goats while they chew knotweed all over Pittsburgh.

~Lainey

P.S. No bees were harmed during the creation of this book.

OTHER STORM SISTERS BOOKS

Bridges and Bitters series

Fireball: An Enemies to Lovers Romance (Sam and AJ)

Liquid Courage: A Marriage in Crisis Romance (Chloe and Teddy)

Speed Rail: A Single Dad Romance (Piper and Cash)

Last Call: A Marriage of Convenience Romance (Esther and Koa)

Planted and Plowed series

Against the Grain (Eila and Ben)

The Burgh and the Bees (Eden and Nate)

Yule Be Sorry (Eliza and Reed)

Sappy Go Lucky (Eva and Asher)

Since You've Bean Gone (Ethan and Lia) *part of the Farm 2 Forking series

www.ingramcontent.com/pod-product-compliance
Lightning Source LLC
Chambersburg PA
CBHW032236190726
48289CB00007BA/2414